· THE LONG PATH TO WISDOM ·

ALSO BY JAN-PHILIPP SENDKER

The Art of Hearing Heartbeats

A Well-Tempered Heart

Jan-Philipp Sendker

WITH

Lorie Karnath

AND

Jonathan Sendker

Translated from the German by
LISA LIESENER AND KEVIN WILIARTY

· THE ·

Long Path

· TO ·

Wisdom

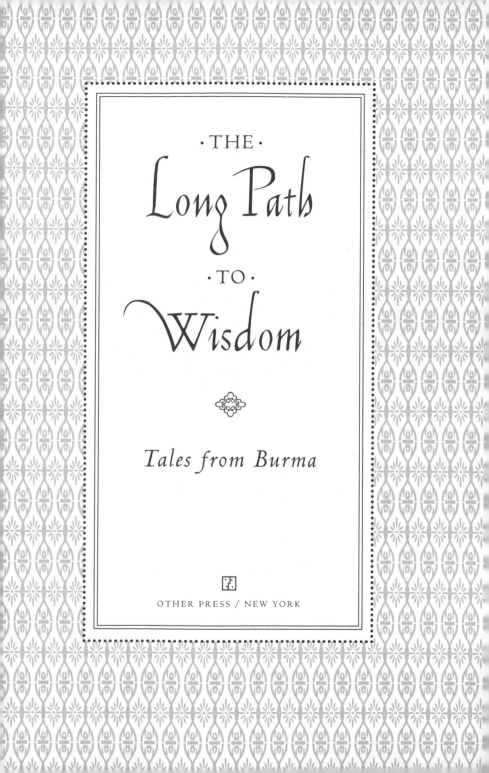

Tales from Burma

OTHER PRESS / NEW YORK

Production editor: Yvonne E. Cárdenas
Text Designer: Jennifer Daddio
This book was set in Centaur MT and Tagliente by
Alpha Design & Composition of Pittsfield, NH

1 3 5 7 9 10 8 6 4 2

Library of Congress Cataloging-in-Publication Data

Names: Sendker, Jan-Philipp, author. | Karnath, Lorie, author. |
Sendker, Jonathan, 1997– author. | Liesener, Lisa, translator. |
Wiliarty, Kevin, translator.
Title: The long path to wisdom : tales from Burma / Jan-Philipp Sendker ; with Lorie Karnath and Jonathan Sendker ; translated from the German by Lisa Liesener and Kevin Wiliarty.
Other titles: Geheimnis des alten Mönches. English.
Description: New York : Other Press, 2018. | "Originally published in German as Das Geheimnis des alten Mönches : Märchen und Fabeln aus Burma in 2017 by Karl Blessing Verlag, Munich"—Title page verso.
Identifiers: LCCN 2018003774 (print) | LCCN 2018018171 (ebook) |
ISBN 9781590519653 (Ebook) | ISBN 9781590519646 (paperback)
Subjects: LCSH: Folk literature, Burmese. | Fairy tales—Burma. |
BISAC: LITERARY COLLECTIONS / Asian. | FICTION / Fairy Tales, Folk Tales, Legends & Mythology. | FICTION / Short Stories (single author).
Classification: LCC GR309 (ebook) | LCC GR309 .S4613 2018 (print) |
DDC 398.209591—dc23
LC record available at https://lccn.loc.gov/2018003774

FOR

our parents

ontents

Preface   *xiii*

My Burma   *1*

The Little Boy and the Tiger   *35*

The Old Monk's Secret   *41*

The Four Marionettes   *45*

How the People of Bagan Started to Lie   *53*

The Sorrowbird   *57*

Five Silver Coins   *61*

The Skylark's Revenge   *65*

Saw Min Kyi and the Ruby   *71*

The Night the Moon Fell into the Well   *77*

Little Monkey Goes Looking for Trouble   *79*

The Farmer's Revenge   *83*

The Fisherman and His Wife   *87*

The Pious Queen   *91*

Nan Kyar Hae and the Guardian Spirit   95

A Battle Between Two Sculptors   97

The Village of Endless Sermons   101

The Long Journey   105

On Gratitude   115

The Traveling Threesome   121

How the Hare Became a Judge   125

Mouse and Elephant   133

How the Thrush Lost Her Colorful Plumage   135

The Just King   143

The Blacksmith's Children   147

The Little Snail   153

A Troop of Monkeys and One Greedy Neighbor   155

Nan Ying and Her Little Brother   159

The Fear Virus   165

On the Rationality of Astrology   169

On Sharing   173

Life's Many Tribulations   177

The Power of Karma   189

The Boy with the Harp   197

The Honest Merchant   203

The Magic Comb   205

A Mother's Warning   209

The Timid Son 213

The Grateful Serpent 219

The Starving Orphans 225

The Flood 227

The Wise Teacher and His Student Maung Pauk Kyaing 231

The Omen 241

How to Spell "Buffalo" 251

The Tale of Two Merchants 255

The White Crow and Love 259

Mu Yeh Peh and the Wages of Love 271

The Beautiful Woman and the Lazy Dimwit 275

The Fisherman's Reward 283

The Best Storyteller 287

The Crocodile and the Monkey 295

The Clever Monkeys 299

Three Women and One Man 305

The Story of the Father and His Son, Or
Where the Wind and Water Got Their Power 313

The Long Path to Wisdom 323

Epilogue 331

Acknowledgments 345

Preface

When the American author Lorie Karnath approached me with the idea of collaborating on a book of Burmese folk tales, fables, and parables, I knew right away that I was interested.

Since 1995 I had visited the former British colony dozens of times, first as a journalist, later as an author. Time and time again during my research for the novels *The Art of Hearing Heartbeats* and *A Well-Tempered Heart* I came across stories from the realm of fairy tales and legends. They piqued my curiosity because their often moving narratives exposed the rich mythologies of the various ethnicities of Burma, the spirituality of its people, and the impact of centuries of Buddhist thought. Monks and monasteries figured prominently, as did the firmly rooted belief in reincarnation. I was surprised how often characters would die only to return in a next life, either to right wrongs or to wreak havoc.

Some tales had no apparent moral or were so alien, so bizarre, that I found them impossible to classify. Others reminded me of the fairy tales of my own childhood except that monkeys, tigers, elephants, and crocodiles stood in for hedgehogs, donkeys, or geese. The lessons they attempted to convey resembled those of the Brothers Grimm or of Hans Christian Andersen, and they highlighted the great extent to which all the world's cultures draw upon a universal font of human wisdom.

Lorie Karnath is no less acquainted with Burma and its people than I. She was there for the first time in the early nineties, a time when the military regime viewed all foreigners with suspicion, when travel was much more complicated than it is today, and when she often found herself getting around by oxcart or horse-drawn wagon. Since then she has explored Burma, its stories, and its culture at great length. She has made many excursions to the various provinces, always engaging intensively with the country's tales and legends. Lorie has already published several essays on Burma as well as the book *Architecture in Burma: Moments in Time*.

Even as the idea for this book was taking shape, my son Jonathan happened to be living in Nyaung Shwe, a small city on the banks of Inle Lake in Shan State, where he and a friend were working as volunteers teaching English in two orphanages. He was eager to participate in the project, and together with Janek Mattheus he set out to find still more tales. During the five months they spent in Burma, Jonathan and Janek canvassed neighborhoods, schools, monasteries, and restaurants, and they came back with notebooks full to bursting.

Further research led us to the bookshops of Yangon, where we tracked down out-of-print volumes and discovered fables and legends in tattered schoolbooks.

And so the present work is very much a team effort. Each of us gathered stories and then wrote up the finest of them. I edited the collection and provided an introduction and epilogue. In the process I have taken care to preserve the narrative voices of my two coauthors so that the texts vary in their style, tempo, and length.

On the not infrequent occasions where we encountered multiple versions of the same tale, we sometimes selected one of them and other times knitted them together. More frequently still we would hear a tale for which—despite several inquiries—we could find no title. In these cases we invented one of our own.

We quickly abandoned our original intention to organize the tales and fables under rubrics such as "Love," "Envy," or "Faith." The texts are too nuanced and varied; it would have been an artificial classification, and it would not have done justice to the material.

Some of these tales will bring a smile to your face; others will move you, trouble you, or make you think.

One thing is certain: The following pages represent a journey into another world, a world sometimes alien, sometimes quite familiar. As authors we have learned from this project that—all cultural and historical differences aside, all exoticism and foreignness notwithstanding—there is much more binding the people of the world together than keeping them apart.

Jan-Philipp Sendker, April 2017

My Burma

· · · · · · · · · · · · · · · · · ·

The first time I heard of the magic of Burma—its beauty, its friendly people, their spirituality and superstitions—I was on a street corner in Kobe surrounded by rubble. A ruinous earthquake had devastated the city. Together with the American photographer Greg Davis I was traveling around Japan as the Asia correspondent for Germany's *Stern* magazine and reporting on the natural disaster. Countless fires still burned in the city, columns of smoke rose from the wreckage, people wandered aimlessly through the streets in search of missing family members. We were both completely exhausted; the experiences of the preceding days had taken their toll. I desperately needed a break.

Greg had been in Burma not long before. Maybe we were looking for solace amid the destruction, suffering, and death. Maybe he was just hoping to offer a momentary distraction with stories from some other place and time. Whatever the case, Greg suddenly started telling me about Burma. He had traveled half the globe as a photographer, but Burma was like no other country he had ever seen—untouched by Western consumerism, inhabitants brimming with curiosity and hospitality toward strangers, hardly a car or television, Southeast Asian villages, cities, and landscapes as they had been fifty or a hundred years ago.

To my ears it sounded like some kind of Shangri-la, and at some point I found myself longing to travel there.

It was not easy to persuade *Stern* to send me there. The former British colony was on no one's radar at that time. In 1962 a junta of generals had seized power in a military coup and through incompetence, corruption, and mismanagement they had driven the once prosperous country into bankruptcy. The opposition leader Aung San Suu Kyi was under house arrest, thousands of political prisoners had been incarcerated, and the military had put a bloody end to the student protests in 1988, during which several thousand people lost their lives. The West responded with sanctions. Burma, lately renamed Myanmar by order of the dictators, was politically and economically isolated.

Nor was Burma on the tourist map of the world. For decades the longest visa, when you could get one, was good only for seven days, too short a time to take in a country the size of France. But the government had declared 1996 the "Year of Tourism," and I wanted to write a piece on how this isolated country was preparing for the throng of visitors it was hoping to attract.

The flight from Bangkok to Yangon took only about an hour, but almost as soon as we landed I realized that I had traveled at least fifty years back in time.

Ours was the only plane on the runway. The single-story terminal was about the size of a small supermarket. The bus that was supposed to take us from the plane to the arrivals area stood derelict beside the airstrip, one door hanging askew. It wasn't going anywhere.

Neither was the luggage belt.

A dozen or so taxi drivers waited by the exit for the few passengers. Every one of them wore a white shirt, a longyi (the Burmese variant on a sarong), and a friendly smile. One driver reached for my bag, which I reluctantly relinquished. He led me to his vehicle, a dented old Toyota with no dashboard. The engine turned over on the third try.

We drove slowly into the city. There were almost no cars or traffic lights. People were on foot, children played in the streets, cooking fires burned in courtyards and alleys. There were no advertisements, no neon lights, no skyscrapers, precious few shops. Our route took us past old teak villas, monasteries, and pagodas. No sign of the world I had left behind just an hour's flight away. At some point I felt so disoriented that I asked the driver whether there was a McDonald's in the city.

He considered this for a long time. Eventually he turned to me and asked: "Might he perhaps be Scottish?"

The famous Shwedagon Pagoda glinted in the evening sun as we drove past. The driver took his hands briefly off the wheel and bowed his head.

It was hot and humid. With temperatures topping a hundred degrees, May is the hottest month in Burma. Sweat ran down my brow and neck; my shirt clung to my body. I asked whether the taxi had a fan or even an air conditioner. Of course it did! Could he perhaps turn it on? No. Regretfully, it was broken.

Eventually we stopped in front of a hotel from the British colonial era where George Orwell purportedly once spent the night. It was early evening; the streets were full of people. Men and women sat in front of houses perched on stools and little benches, drinking tea, fan-ning themselves, chatting, laughing. I brought my bag straight to my room and could hardly wait to explore this strange, remarkable city.

Everywhere I went people welcomed me with their eyes: surprised, friendly, curious. Now and then someone would speak to me, usually an older gentleman: "Where are you from, sir?" they wanted to know in accents that sounded British or Indian.

Supposing that they were hoping to sell me some useless trinket or other, I replied, "Germany," then hurried on. Until it dawned on me that there was almost nothing to sell. These men had been interested only in a bit of conversation, delighted to see a foreigner, someone to speak English with.

All at once there was a loud popping sound and everything went dark. Power outage. A daily annoyance, as I would soon learn. But the people were accustomed to it and knew just what to do. They lit candles. These days generators would spring into action everywhere, and their dull droning would fill the streets, but back then they were almost unheard of. Within minutes the whole neighborhood was alight with candles. From windowsills, doorsteps, sidewalks, and teahouses they bathed the city in a magical light. With no cars on the road and no electricity, there were few sounds besides the human voices. Laughter. Whispering. Children shouting. Singing.

It was the singing that took me by surprise. I would follow the notes wherever they led me—to a gateway or a courtyard on the banks of a river. I was always met by the same scene: a young couple sitting together, the man serenading the woman. Later I would learn that this is a Burmese courting tradition.

I thought of Greg and was filled with gratitude.

The next day, perspiring, I wandered aimlessly through the city. Eventually I came upon a house with these faded words above the door: "Bagan Book Store—English Books." Not knowing any Burmese and having no contacts in the city, I thought this might be a good place to make a start.

It was tiny, not two hundred square feet, with wooden shelves, homemade by the looks of them, piled nearly to the ceiling with old books. In the middle of the room an old man squatted by a flat table in the breeze of a lethargic fan. He wore a faded longyi and a ragged white under-shirt. He looked up and asked what I was looking for. Just browsing, I replied.

He nodded and returned to his work. The book in front of him was in a pitiful state, the pages tattered and full of holes. To the side stood two little jars. One held tiny bits of paper, the other glue. With tweezers the old bookseller would fish a bit of paper out of the first jar, dip it in the glue, and then use it to patch one of the holes in the pages of the book. Taking a black pen and a loupe, he would then ink in the missing letters. The book was at least three hundred pages, and he was not very far into it. Little beads of sweat would build up on his brow, and he would wipe them away with a cloth. It was hotter in the shop than it had been on the street.

On the floor stood several piles of books, all in a similarly deplorable state.

I looked around at the bookcases. There were a dozen paperbacks, light reading that travelers had probably left behind. Most of the space was taken up by books about Burma, the country's history and culture, its traditions, its art, its animals and plants.

"Are you looking for anything in particular?"

"No."

"Is this your first time here?" He spoke perfect English, with a British accent.

"Yes. Where did you learn to speak English so well?" I inquired.

"I learned it from the English." Noticing my amazement, he added: "But that was long ago."

I looked at the book spread out before him. "May I ask what you are doing?"

"I am restoring a book."

"How long does it take you to do a single volume?"

"Two or three months," he replied.

I nodded. The heat was getting to me, and I asked if I might sit down for a minute. He brought over a stool. For some time, in silence, I watched him work.

"Would you like something to drink?" he asked suddenly.

"Very much."

And so the old bookseller rose and disappeared into a room at the back of the shop. Moments later he returned with a thermos of tea and two cups. Gingerly we started a conversation, interrupted by long pauses, and we continued it over a number of days. Each afternoon I would pay him a visit, lingering somewhat longer each time, while he told me the story of his family. They had once belonged to the country's wealthy and educated, but they had lost everything in the military dictatorship that followed the coup in 1962. Everything except the books. "Soldiers take little interest in literature," he said with a quick smile. "Fortunately."

To preserve the books from decay he restored them, copied and bound them, then sold the copies to some of the rare tourists, diplomats, or businessmen who found themselves in Burma in those days. But truth be told, he saw himself primarily as the guardian of a treasure he wanted to pass along to future generations. He pointed to a little girl playing in the street. She would sometimes run through the shop and disappear into the apartment at the back. She was his granddaughter. "If I don't look after the books, she'll never have her own chance to read them."

The more we talked, and the farther I roamed in Yangon, the keener my interest in this country and its history grew.

When it came time for me to travel farther north, he handed me a parting gift: a book he himself had restored, copied, and bound. Because I was such an extraordinarily curious person with so many questions about Burma, he said. I would find some of the answers in this book, he supposed.

I was touched and grateful. I carefully leafed through the first few pages. *The Soul of a People.* Published in London in 1902. As a reporter I did not generally have much time to read books that were published a hundred years ago. Slightly disappointed, I closed the book.

"Thank you," I said. "It's rather old, isn't it?"

He furrowed his brow in thought, as if it had never occurred to him. "True enough," he answered after a pause.

"But no matter; the soul of a people does not change so quickly."

I stood in the late afternoon with hundreds of other passengers on a platform at the main train station in Yangon, an imposing building from the fifties, built in traditional Burmese style. I intended to catch a train to Mandalay, about four hundred miles away. The "night train to Mandalay" had a romantic ring to it. According to the timetable it would take twelve hours. More likely fourteen, the bookseller had warned. Or eighteen. Or twenty-four. Depending on the condition of the track, the vagaries of the weather, and a host of other unpredictable factors.

We pulled out of the station right on time in the early evening, and the first two or three hours of the journey were among the finest I have spent on any train. We lumbered along the rails at ten, maybe twenty miles an hour, sometimes even at a walk. Warm breezes drifted through the open windows. Street vendors scurried up and hopped on, then ambled through the cars hawking curries, tea, or soup in plastic bags, fruit, crackers, water. At some point they would just jump back off again.

A picturesque Asian landscape rolled past my window. Rice paddies, little rivers, children riding water buffalo. The sunset behind palm trees.

It was the ideal speed for the human senses. I heard the voices of children playing. The scent of open cooking fires drifted through the cars, preparation for the evening meal. Any time we approached a river the heat relented, only slightly, but still perceptibly.

But then night fell, and there was nothing more to see. The wooden bench I was sitting on grew harder by the hour; the unbearable heat and humidity persisted. Sleep was out of the question. By hour ten I was completely drained; after twelve hours I wanted nothing more in the world than to be done with the "night train to Mandalay."

At the next stop I grabbed my pack and stepped out. Dawn found me standing at the train station in Thazi surrounded by hundreds of sleeping travelers—curled up on the platform, the baggage carts, the stairs. Waiting for some connection that would eventually arrive. Timetables in Burma, I would learn, offered only rough approximations.

In front of the station was one of those white Toyotas that often serve as taxis. A man was sleeping inside. A few yards away a snack cart had already opened for business. A kettle hung over a fire, and the first customers crouched groggily on stools to sip their tea. I sat down beside them, ordered a Burmese tea, and waited for the driver to wake.

A few hours later we were on the road to Kalaw. I had picked up two potential contacts from a diplomat in Yangon. I was looking for Tommy and Father Angelo. Just ask anyone.

Father Angelo was well over eighty, an Italian missionary who had lived in Burma for decades. He introduced me to Tommy Ezdani, a short man, about fifty, with an almost delicate frame who looked me over full of curiosity. He wore a yellow bath towel that he had wrapped around his head into something like a turban. He caught my dubious expression and explained, amused, that it was the headwear of the Pa-O people, an ethnic minority that lived in Shan State. He had just returned from a visit to one of their villages.

We immediately hit it off. During the following weeks he would accompany me on various excursions. Even today nearly all of my trips to Burma include a visit to Tommy in Shan State. Though born in Kalaw, Tommy was a Pashtun. English colonial rulers had relocated his grandfather from Afghanistan to Burma. Even as a child he had frequently accompanied his grandfather, a doctor, to the surrounding villages of the Pa-O, the Palaung, the Shan, and the Karen, so that he grew up learning the languages of the various ethnic groups that live in the mountains encircling Kalaw. When we met, he had only recently founded an aid organization that was building schools, wells, and bridges in remote settlements.

After a few days in Kalaw he asked me if I wouldn't like to visit some of the villages with him. We would walk to our destination and spend the night there; I would see a completely different side of Burma.

A few hours into the hike we ran into a woman whom Tommy obviously knew well. She was gaunt, with long arms and big, sturdy hands. On her back she carried a sizable bundle of firewood that she had gathered in the forest. The two got into a lively conversation, but all the while she kept a sharp eye on me. She was scrutinizing me, not antagonistically, more out of curiosity, sizing me up. Eventually she approached me and wanted to touch my arms. I backed away and asked Tommy what she wanted from me.

"She wants to marry you."

I looked at him, confused.

"She's offering five cows for you. I told her that was too much. You're already thirty-five, after all."

By Burmese standards that was old, he said. The average life expectancy was only fifty-three.

But she would not be dissuaded. I looked rather different from the locals. She reckoned I would last longer.

We went our way, and near evening we reached a Pa-O village where Tommy enjoyed considerable popularity. Only a short time earlier he had organized the installation of a pipeline from a water source more than a mile away. Now at least there was a well in the village, and no one had to walk miles for a pail of fresh water. Tommy was acquainted with their language and culture, and he was a frequent and very welcome guest. We were greeted by children who stared at me wide-eyed. Everyone tagged along as we made our way to the village leader. His old teak house stood on stilts. A pig rooted around underneath it.

The man and his family welcomed us warmly, and invited us to spend the night.

That evening we sat around a fire; the family had slaughtered a chicken and prepared a curry in my honor. Of course my plate was piled with the choicest bits, and no one else would eat a thing until I was finished. A Burmese host eats only when the guests have had their fill. The village elders had come, men and women, and they watched my every move with curiosity. Above the crackle of the fire I heard children whispering and giggling in the dark. A baby fussed but settled quickly. An older woman sat close by speaking softly to a circle of children. I could not understand a word she said, but the melody in her voice had a magical quality. I asked Tommy who she was and what she was doing. A grandmother telling her grandchildren a fairy tale, he explained. It was still very much a living tradition in Burma, as I learned on subsequent visits, especially among the ethnic minorities and in the villages.

I had no shortage of questions for my hosts, but at some point it occurred to me that they might have questions of their own.

They discussed it for a while, and eventually someone wanted to know how long it would take me to reach their village. By oxcart.

I tried to estimate the travel time from Hong Kong. One year? Two?

More than a year, I replied.

General amazement. The village leader's wife wanted to know how many suns we have where I come from.

I didn't understand her question.

She spelled it out for me: I would probably not be able to work my fields for three years. One year for the journey out, another for the journey back, and to make the most of such a long trip I would presumably spend a year at my destination. She herself could never afford such a long absence, no matter how hard she worked. My fields must therefore be extraordinarily productive, and that she could explain only if we had multiple suns that shone for more than the usual twelve to fourteen hours.

When it came time to retire for the night my hosts showed me my bed: a paper-thin mat on wooden floorboards. They must have seen from my expression that I was not used to sleeping on the floor. I had not said a word, but they pulled together some blankets and cloths and made them into a mattress. They had me test it several times and were not satisfied until I sank deep into it.

When Tommy and I took our leave the next morning nearly everyone in the village had come to offer their good wishes for the road. They also had a farewell gift for me, as is customary among friends in Burma.

The village leader handed me a sizable sack nearly bursting with black tea. Now, I like to drink tea, but this was more than enough for a lifetime. I thanked them sincerely but suggested that it might be too much of a good thing. Maybe they had a smaller bag or even a pouch?

Of course so much tea was not intended for me alone, they countered; it was for my whole family.

"But I live alone," I told them. It took a while for Tommy's translation to make its way around the entire group.

"Alone?" they asked, astonished.

I nodded.

At no other moment in my life had so many people looked on me with such pity.

Alone.

No one in Burma lives alone. Bachelor or widow, everyone lives among their extended family. You'd have to be a pretty unsavory character before no one wanted to live with you, Tommy would later explain.

In order to break the tension I explained that I was married, but that my wife was still living in New York in order to finish her studies while I lived in Hong Kong, but that I called her every evening if it was at all possible. They passed around this new information. There was some whispering and nodding, and then everyone relaxed and smiled.

"Really every evening?" the village leader asked, doubt in his voice.

I nodded.

"Then you must have a very loud voice."

When I returned to Kalaw almost exactly one year later, Tommy asked me if I had time to hike back to the village with him. He had been there often since our visit. People inquired about me every time, and they would surely be delighted to see me again.

He was not kidding. We had hardly arrived before we were surrounded by a small throng. Everyone wanted to welcome their foreign friend. I had brought balloons and a few toys for the children.

We were invited again to spend the night, but this time the atmosphere was different, joyfully enthusiastic, almost festive. After dinner many more people gathered in the village leader's house than the previous year. We sat in long, cramped rows on the floor in front of a cabinet. It was clear they were planning some sort of dramatic unveiling. At some point our host rose and opened the cabinet doors with a flourish. And there was a television. The military junta had doled out battery-powered televisions, they told me, the better to spread their propaganda. But the people were no fools; they ignored the official broadcasts. There was only one national broadcaster, and once a week they featured a foreign movie. As luck would have it, I had arrived on just the right day.

For the next forty-five minutes we watched an episode of some mindless American detective series. It was set in Los Angeles, and not much happened aside from the continual car crashes, exploding helicopters, and people shooting or stabbing one another. The villagers stared at the screen, stunned, stealing an occasional horrified glance in my direction. I did after all bear a considerable physical resemblance to those perpetrators of nonstop wickedness.

When the show was over, our host rose, turned off the television, closed the cabinet doors, turned to me and regarded me for a long time. I avoided eye contact. Awkward silence filled the room. He cleared his throat.

"If you wish, Jan-Philipp, you may stay here with us. It is much too dangerous where you live."

I did not take their offer, though I have returned to Burma many times since, first as a journalist—twice I was able to visit the former opposition leader and current head of government, Aung San Suu Kyi, in her home—later as a writer doing research for the novels *The Art of Hearing Heartbeats* and *A Well-Tempered Heart*. My fascination deepened with each visit. I gathered impressions and stories and took a growing interest in Burmese folk tales, fables, and legends. Whenever I saw a woman telling stories to her children or grandchildren I would sit down with them if at all possible, and have the stories translated for me. I learned that in their tales, too, animals played an important role, though for them it was of course tigers, elephants, crocodiles, and monkeys.

I was also struck by the fact that the evil mother-in-law often made an appearance. The wicked stepmother, on the other hand, was not nearly as prominent as in our tales.

Whenever I stayed overnight at a monastery I would ask the monks about Buddhist fables and parables. I heard many stories about the Buddha's wisdom, but I also heard about how difficult it can be even for a monk to apply these teachings in everyday life. The story of the two sculptors beating one another to death (p. 97) is a case in point. Likewise the story of the young monk in "The Long Path to Wisdom" when he feels compelled to choose between the Buddha and his parents (p. 323).

Years later, while traveling through the country researching my first novel, I resolved to begin collecting Burmese folk tales so that I might incorporate some of them into the book. And so I spent many evenings sitting around campfires with women who, somewhat perplexed by a foreigner's interest, told me tales, legends, and fables. Many of these stories reminded me of my own childhood. There is, for instance, a Burmese version of the story of the tortoise and the hare, except that a turtle outsmarts a conceited and overconfident horse.

Many of the legends describe the origins of the numerous mythical characters, ghosts, and deities.

At times I was appalled by the cruelty of certain stories, such as "The Flood" (p. 227), where an entire village commits an atrocious crime for which they must atone. When I considered "Hansel and Gretel" and "The Wolf and the Seven Little Goats," however, I recalled that not all of the Grimms' tales were for the faint of heart.

Many stories tell of dismal sorrow, such as the tale of "The Starving Orphans" (p. 225), in which two siblings starve to death and are doomed to this day to scour the country in the shape of birds, searching for one another.

I was strongly reminded of Hans Christian Andersen's tales, especially the fate of his "Little Match Girl," whose poverty and loneliness reliably moved me to tears as a child.

While working on *The Art of Hearing Heartbeats* I determined to incorporate the gorgeous love story "The Tale of the Prince, the Princess, and the Crocodile" into the broader narrative. I had heard it from several women beside many a campfire. The main character of the novel, Tin Win, is a Burmese man sent by his family in the 1940s to New York City, where he lives for many years. In the book he tells his little daughter, Julia, Burmese fairy tales, and this is her favorite. Tin Win's American wife does not know what to make of the legends from her husband's homeland. She finds them "confused and bizarre...without any moral and completely unsuitable for children." Julia, on the other hand, loves these myths and their marvelous settings, so different from the stories she hears from her mother. The present volume represents a small selection of Tin Win's repertoire.

The major themes of humanity come into play: Love. Faith. Greed. Trust. Betrayal. Forgiveness.

Good does not always triumph. Many of the tales are informed by a deep fatalism, others by a longing for justice or the magical power of love. They give us a glimpse into an unfamiliar, sometimes even exotic realm of thought and beliefs, only to strike us in surprising ways as utterly familiar in their humanity just a few pages later.

It would be misleading to say that the people of Burma are superstitious. Superstition smacks of mummery, naïve gullibility, or childish irrationality.

Yet many Burmese people take it absolutely for granted that the stars exert influence over human lives, that there are dates and days that bring luck and others that invite calamity. They would not understand how anyone could doubt it. It is such an integral part of their everyday lives and their worldview that it requires neither mention nor explanation. Again and again during my investigations I asked people whether they were superstitious. With deep conviction they denied it, categorically, only to tell me a moment later of a *nat*, a guardian spirit, who lived in a tree in their garden and to whom they made a daily offering. Or of their last consultation with an astrologer.

During my first visit to Yangon, a young man drove me through the city in a vehicle that was barely roadworthy, with a steering wheel on the right in a country that drives on the right, a circumstance that made passing difficult, even life-threatening. He told me that many years ago the traffic direction had been switched from left to right overnight on the advice of an astrologer. I did not get the impression that he found this at all shocking.

Stuck to his dashboard was a black-and-white photo of a young woman with an infant in her arms. Curious, I asked who it was. He smiled proudly and explained that it was his wife and baby daughter. She was four months old, but, alas, he saw far too little of her because he had to work so much. He had big debts.

I was surprised that such a young man already had creditors and asked whether he had taken a loan to buy the car.

Not for that, he said, but for his daughter's birth. An astrologer had calculated the best day, even the best hour for the birth. Not wanting to leave anything to chance, they had elected to have a cesarean. And that was very, very expensive.

For me that was the beginning of a journey into an utterly unfamiliar world populated by spirits, ghosts, demons, and other mystical apparitions. A world full of cryptic rituals and magical numerology, where it is not uncommon for an astrologer, an exorcist, or a medium to have the final say.

I encountered superstition on a daily basis, often when I least expected it. One time I was traveling with a Burmese friend, and we were lamenting the notoriously bad state of the pothole-ridden roads. Suddenly the road transformed beneath us into a four-lane highway, impeccably surfaced, with good signage and a painted center line. Soon enough the miracle was over, and we were back to the accustomed bumps and jolts. I asked in confusion why that stretch of road had suddenly been in such good condition. My friend explained that an astrologer had advised the regional military commander to build something in order to court the goodwill of the stars. He would otherwise run the risk of a demotion. It must be something that served the common good. It should have a connection with traffic and involve the numbers four and five. The general commissioned the construction of this four-lane road for a length of exactly five hundred meters.

I wondered aloud whether it had done any good.

My friend shrugged. The commander was still in office, at any rate.

On that drive he told me of various political decisions that were guided by the advice of astrologers. Much to the consternation of the British, it was an astrologer who had determined the time for the Burmese independence ceremony. It had to take place on January 4, 1948, at 4:20 in the morning. In this case, at least, the numbers do not seem to have brought the country much luck.

The severe political unrest of 1987 seems also to have been unleashed by an astrologer and a general under his sway, in this case Ne Win, the most powerful man in the country. Overnight the twenty-five-, thirty-five-, and seventy-five-kyat bank notes were demonetized in favor of ninety- and forty-five-kyat notes. An astrologer had apparently prophesied doom for the dictator; only his lucky number nine could improve his fate. So Ne Win saw to it that these numbers came into the widest circulation possible. He did not allow people to exchange their worthless bills for the new ones, so many people lost their savings. Vehement protests ensued, which the military brutally suppressed.

Even the official renaming of the country from Burma to Myanmar was instigated by an astrologer. And it was announced on May 27. Two plus seven is nine.

Years later and quite unexpectedly the junta declared that they would construct a new national capital, Naypyidaw, in the interior. Within a few years and at the cost of hundreds of millions of U.S. dollars, the impoverished country had conjured a new seat of government out of thin air. The generals have never given a plausible public explanation of their sudden need for some capital other than Yangon. Apparently the rationale for this decision, too, lies in the prophecies of an astrologer. He strongly urged the rulers to relocate, lest catastrophe befall the land. He even set the date and time for the commencement of the transition: November 6 at 6:37 a.m.

As part of my research for *The Art of Hearing Heartbeats* I decided to visit an astrologer in Kalaw. In my travels I had often seen the important role astrology played in the lives of the Burmese; now I wanted to experience for myself what a visit to an astrologer was like, so that I could later write about it.

My friend Winston told me there was a highly regarded astrologer in Kalaw. People from far and wide sought his advice in all matters of life. Whether a couple was suited for marriage, what was the most auspicious date for a wedding, or the most favorable day for a move or a journey. He could reportedly interpret the stars like few others.

Off we went. To this day I have never had much interest in horoscopes or astrology. I would occasionally read my horoscope in the newspaper. When it was positive, I believed it; when negative, I considered it superstitious nonsense. I had never visited a tarot reader or fortune-teller or even had any interest in doing so. When people told me about predictions that had come true for friends, I would smile and dismiss them as bunk.

Winston brought me to an old teak house on stilts. We climbed a rickety staircase whose worn steps attested to heavy traffic over the years. We were met by an old man with white, close-cropped hair. He wore a threadbare undershirt and a longyi and offered us a seat on the floor. As we sat there, my eyes wandered around the room. On the wooden walls hung two posters in Burmese script that explained something about the various heavenly bodies. Between the posters were some calendar pages with mountainous landscapes. There was a bookcase crammed with tattered volumes and notebooks. In front of him, on the wooden floor, lay a small slate. He poured tea for us and asked us the reason for our visit. Because I was more interested in the atmosphere and ritual than in the predictions, I asked him, off the top of my head, a couple of innocent questions about my past and my future. He wanted to know the place of my birth, the exact time, the day and the year. He made notes, consulted some of the tattered books, and started calmly to write. Several minutes passed during which he calculated, wrote down combinations of numbers, wiped them away with an old cloth, added new ones. Finally he looked up and started to talk. The first few sentences were fairly general, but all correct. I was curious now, so I told him that I had been a journalist but was now an author, and that I wanted in the future to work exclusively as a novelist.

The astrologer foretold great success. I had nothing to worry about.

Of course I was happy to hear that, but on a whim, or perhaps in order to expose him as a fraud, I gave him the place, date, and time of birth for a young girl in my family who suffered from a rare eye disorder.

He asked for patience and resumed the calculations that to me seemed so outlandish. Eventually he put the slate aside and said: "This child will be a source of concern for her parents."

Nothing odd about that, I thought, especially in the West. Could he perhaps be more precise?

"Health problems."

I was briefly irritated. Of course; many children get sick. Could he say more?

He returned to his calculations, consulted more notebooks. In the end he looked at me gravely: "Health problems in the head."

I felt queasy. "Could you say more?" I asked quietly.

Yet again he turned to his inscrutable calculations.

"The eyes."

I sat there in shock. There was no way that this old man in the mountains in Shan State could know anything about this child's illness. And yet it was so.

How? Where did he get his information? It was no mere chance; his interpretations were too precise for that. So what else was there?

To this day I have no explanation. I would not say that I embraced a new belief in astrology. If that were so, then I would feel compelled to consult with the astrologer in Kalaw before every important decision. Yet neither can I simply go on as if that experience had never happened and claim that I do not believe in it at all. There are, I have learned during my travels in Burma, mysterious things between heaven and earth, things we do not understand and to which some people have more access than others. Or as U Ba puts it in *The Art of Hearing*

Heartbeats: "Not all truths are explicable...And not all explicable things are true."

Intrigued by that first encounter, I have since sought out numerous astrologers, fortune-tellers, and exorcists in Burma, but I have never met another who even came close to providing such precise information.

*Nat*s play a special role in the lives of many Burmese people. I became acquainted with them on my very first visit while riding in a car through the pouring rain in the vicinity of Bagan.

We were rattling along a rural route in a rental car when the driver suddenly stopped under an expansive banyan tree beside a pagoda. He took a wreath of fresh jasmine blossoms that he had just purchased during a rest at a teahouse, got out of the car, and walked to the tree. The rain was drumming on the windshield and roof of the car. But now I was curious, so I followed him. The gnarled trunk with its intertwining offshoots measured several yards across. Between two of the trunk's limbs stood an altar under the shelter of a small corrugated tin roof. On the altar stood the statue of a mythical creature carved in wood and covered generously with gold leaf. It wore magnificent clothes and a sort of tall, pointed crown.

Around it were plates large and small piled with bananas, coconuts, candies, pastries, and cigarettes.

To these offerings my driver added his jasmine wreath, white and green. Here in this tree, he told me, lived a famous *nat*. Every time he passes the tree he makes a small offering so that the *nat* will protect him while driving.

Nat? I asked, uncertain whether I had understood correctly.

He could hardly believe I had never heard of them. They were everywhere, after all. There were spirits for the water, the trees, the air. Many rivers, buildings, pagodas, villages, even individual homes had their own guardian spirits. And then there was the list of thirty-seven especially notable Great *Nats* who were renowned throughout the country, celebrated and revered at countless festivals. Most of them, my driver told me, had previously been humans who met violent deaths. They had sacrificed themselves for others, or they had been slain by devils, rivals, thieves, or other evildoers. After death they had ascended into the divine company of the *nats*. It would constitute gross negligence not to make regular offerings to them.

Many years later in a village, I was taken to see an old woman, of whom it was said that she could communicate with the *nats* and that she could call on them for help in all kinds of situations. There was a line of clients sitting and waiting on the steps to her house. They included a woman and her daughter wondering whether the spirits could aid them in their search for a husband for the young woman. There was also a man looking for advice in a dispute with his neighbor. Half an hour later it was our turn. The astonished woman greeted us and invited us in. No foreigner had ever sought her advice. The room felt like a curious mix of junk shop, temple, and grocery. In one corner were boxes of crackers, little bags of rice, nuts, packaged noodles intermingled with toothpaste, soap, laundry detergent, a few bottles of soda, and cooking oil. It looked as if she operated mostly on a barter system.

On numerous altars stood gilded wooden carvings of *nats*. All about them lay offerings. A coconut, bananas, cigarettes, candles, bottled beers, flasks of Burmese whiskey. Many of the figures were draped in pink, red, or yellow fabrics. Others wore wooden necklaces or garlands of fresh jasmine. A brightly colored, flickering string of lights framed a poster of the Shwedagon Pagoda.

We sat on the linoleum floor. A handful of curious onlookers came in from the kitchen and courtyard. They sat down with us, watching us closely.

The woman closed her eyes for a few seconds. She was small, almost dainty, and she must have been about eighty, but as soon as the talk turned to *nats* she radiated energy.

The price for the consultation was thirty thousand kyat, half a month's salary for a teacher. I set the money on the floor between us. She wrapped a pink cloth around her head, put on a scarf, and settled into her work. She dug a few shells out of a can and threw them to the floor, reading them as if they were dice. She repeated this a second and third time. Then for some minutes she struck herself on her head and upper body, mumbling something, stretching out her arms, swinging them through the air, speaking loudly, then whispering again. After a while she announced ceremoniously that the spirit of the *nat* was now in our midst. She lit a cigarette, took a few puffs, and then passed it around like a joint. Next she shook a can of beer long and energetically, opened it, and let the warm contents spray like a fountain through the room. She took a slug and then passed the can around without a word. When I hesitated to put it to my lips she gave me a stern look that let me know I had no choice but to partake.

As soon as the can was empty she threw grains of rice around the room as a further offering to the *nat*. She rolled up the bills I had put on the floor and stuck them in her headband. She shook a handful of rice into a bowl and tossed it to me unexpectedly. I caught it without spilling a grain. She smiled, pleased.

The *nat*, a patron of teachers, artists, and authors, was favorably inclined toward me. I need not worry about my next books.

Though delighted to hear it, I remained unconvinced by her performance—not so the Burmese in attendance. They nodded devoutly and looked at me overjoyed. Good fortune was obviously smiling on me. It would not have occurred to any of them to dismiss the visitation as silly hocus-pocus or a scam.

In very different ways several tales and legends in this book thematize astrology, spirits, superstition in Burma, and the power of the stars.

Again and again it is spirits, good or evil, who either rescue people in need or put them in harm's way. In one story a prince falls in love with a *nat* who puts him to a severe test. In another, two monks get into a vehement argument about whether the stars influence human lives or not.

Interestingly, the tale provides no answer to that question.

The Little Boy and the Tiger

In a village on the edge of the jungle there once lived a young boy named Po. He was an inquisitive child who loved nothing more than roaming through the wilderness, climbing trees, and befriending the animals. One of Po's dearest companions was a tiger, and the two played together for hours on end. The boy loved the tiger, and the tiger was genuinely fond of the boy, but his affection also had an ulterior motive. The tiger secretly hoped that Po might one night sneak him into the village, where he could help himself to one of the fat, juicy cows.

One day, as they were resting on the bank of a small river, the tiger decided the time had come to reveal his secret desire. "My dear friend, now that we have spent so much time together, might I ask you for a favor?"

"Of course!" replied the boy.

"Can you take me with you into your village tonight after dark?"

"I can't do *that!*" replied the boy, startled. "You know how the villagers fear you. They loathe tigers and would try to catch or even kill you!"

The tiger was disappointed. "I am not afraid of the villagers. If you won't help me, then I will just go by myself."

That evening, Po watched anxiously at the village entrance for his friend. As soon as he saw the tiger approaching, he implored him to return to the jungle. "Please! Go back to the forest and hide! They will kill you!"

"Then help me."

"I can't," Po replied. Then, hearing his mother and father calling, he pleaded: "I have to go home now. Please, my friend, stay away from our village!"

The next morning, the whole village was abuzz with news of the happenings of the previous night. A tiger from the jungle had stolen into the village and eaten one of the calves. The villagers all feared that he would return the next night to devour yet another of their precious cows or pigs, so they decided to set a trap for him.

When Po heard this, he ran into the jungle to search for his friend. He found the tiger, his belly full, happily dozing under a tree.

"My dear Tiger," he cried frantically, "You mustn't ever return to our village! The farmers are building a trap for you!"

The tiger smiled and waved a dismissive paw. "Don't worry, little friend. The villagers are too stupid. They will never catch me."

That night the tiger sneaked back into the village and walked right into the trap. The next morning, the farmers found the furious tiger roaring loudly as he paced back and forth in the bamboo cage. The entire village gathered in awe before the cage to marvel at the magnificent beast. Since no one had the courage to kill him, they decided simply to leave the tiger in the cage until he perished on his own of hunger and thirst. That evening, the little boy crept sorrowfully to the cage to visit his friend.

"Why didn't you listen to me?" he asked, distraught.

"Oh, my dear Po, I was foolish. I admit it. But now I need you to free me. If you don't, I will starve to death."

"I'm sorry. I can't do that."

"Please! You are my only hope."

"There is no way, Tiger. My parents, no, the whole village would beat me to a pulp!"

Evening after evening Po visited the tiger. With each passing day the boy felt worse as he watched his cherished friend slowly waste away. On the seventh day, he could bear it no longer. That night, after his mother and father were asleep, Po slipped silently out of his hut and ran to the cage.

"In the name of our friendship," he declared, throwing open the door with a flourish. The tiger sprang out of the cage and reared up before the boy, flashing his teeth hungrily.

"I am famished and much too drained to hunt. I am just going to have to eat you."

Po recoiled in horror. "You can't be serious!? You ought to be grateful to me for freeing you!"

"Don't be ridiculous," growled the tiger. "I owe you nothing. I am hungry!"

The two argued fiercely until the boy finally persuaded the animal to let an impartial judge settle their dispute.

They went into the jungle, where they eventually found the skull of an ox. They each told their side of the story and asked the skull to adjudicate. The skull listened quietly and then replied without hesitation: "No one owes anyone anything. For years I toiled in my master's fields.

I pulled his carts up and down hills through the slickest mud, in the hottest sun and heaviest rains. I went with him to the market, pulling or carrying everything he required. Yet when I became old and weak, he slaughtered and ate me. The tiger owes the boy nothing. He may eat him."

"My argument exactly," roared the tiger, teeth bared. Trembling, Po begged for a second opinion. "All right," hissed the tiger, "but only because it is you who is asking."

They turned to a large banyan tree. "You are old and wise," said Po. "Please decide which of us is right."

The tree listened attentively as they described their disagreement, and then immediately reached a decision. "There is no such thing as owing someone a debt of gratitude. When the hot sun burns down from above, the villagers gather beneath me to rest in the shade of my leaves, and yet they break my branches and steal my flowers. They would chop me down without a second thought if it struck their fancy. Is this how they repay me? Where is the gratitude in that? Let the tiger eat the human child."

The beast approached the boy and opened his mouth wide.

"Please don't," screamed Po. "I have the right to a third judgment!"

"This is your last chance," cried the tiger angrily. "No one may appeal a verdict more than twice."

Shortly thereafter, they met a hare who was highly esteemed in the entire jungle for his shrewdness and wisdom. They told him of their disagreement and asked his opinion.

"Hmm," he answered. "This is a difficult case. Show me exactly where it all started."

It being the middle of the night, they all walked back into Po's village.

"Where were you when this all began?" the hare asked the tiger.

"In the cage."

"Where exactly?"

The tiger trotted back into the cage.

"And you, Po? Lock the door and show me how you opened it."

Po slid the lock back into place.

"Stop!" cried the hare suddenly. "Leave the door closed! I have restored the proper order of things. The tiger is in the cage. The boy is standing outside it. All is just as it was before the argument began, and so it is settled." Without another word, the hare hopped away and was gone. Po turned and ran back to his mother and father as quickly as his legs could carry him.

A few days later the tiger was dead, vanquished by hunger and thirst.

The Old Monk's Secret

There was once an old monk who lived as a hermit on the outskirts of a small village. He had once been a wealthy man but after the death of his wife, he had given up his riches and withdrawn to the forest, where he could meditate undisturbed and devote himself to the teachings of the Enlightened One. The one valuable thing he had secretly kept for himself was a single pot of gold, and this he had hidden under a nearby banyan tree. Though it was well concealed, the monk still worried that the pot of gold might sometime be discovered. If the villagers found it, they would spread the word far and wide that he had not truly renounced all worldly wealth.

The villagers, who knew nothing of his concerns, greatly respected the old monk for his modesty and wisdom and came to the forest often to pay their respects and to bring him offerings.

One day, a farmer and his wife arrived with a plate of fruit and rice cakes. They told the monk of their son, who was now old enough to train as a novice. With heads bowed, they humbly asked the monk to accept the boy as his student. The monk agreed. The next day, they brought him their son, whose name was Moonface, and in the months that followed, both parents came to the forest often to visit their child. Over time, the old monk befriended the couple and came to trust them so much that one day he revealed his secret pot of gold to them. He asked the farmer and his wife to take it home with them and to hide it on their farm. The couple was hesitant at first, but after thinking it over, they agreed.

One day a few weeks later, the farmer came running through the forest in a panic. In his hands, he held the old monk's pot, but the coins inside no longer shimmered yellow. "I cannot explain how it happened," the man declared breathlessly, "but your gold seems to have turned to copper overnight."

The monk ground his teeth angrily, for he knew that the farmer was lying to him. Without betraying his anger, he took back the pot and said: "It is all right. There is nothing to be done."

After that, the monk lay awake night after night contemplating how to get revenge on the dishonest farmer until he finally knew what to do.

The monk began to tame one of the monkeys that lived in the nearby trees. Using the fruit and biscuits that the villagers brought him, he was soon able to teach the animal a few tricks. After a while, the monkey was so tame that he came running when called. To summon him, the monk needed only to cup his hands to his mouth and loudly call out "Moonface!"

The next day, the monk led his student to a spot deep in the forest and instructed him to stay there alone to meditate until the monk returned. He then hurried back to his hut. That very afternoon, the farmer arrived to visit his son.

The old monk called for him loudly: "Moonface!" Almost immediately the monkey came bounding out of the trees.

"That is not my son!" cried the outraged farmer.

"Indeed it is," declared the monk.

"Nonsense! How could a child turn into a monkey?"

A brief smile flashed over the old monk's face. "If gold can turn into copper," he explained, "then a child can also turn into a monkey."

The Four Marionettes

A long, long time ago, in the mountains of Burma, there lived a family of puppet makers. The father, his wife, and their son crafted the most beautiful marionettes, which they sold to children, puppeteers, and circus artists in the nearby villages.

The son, Aung, soon grew to be an ambitious young man who longed to go out into the world. He dreamed of traveling and someday starting his own puppet workshop. He asked his parents for permission to carry out his plan, and after considering his request for a while, they finally consented.

Before he left, his mother packed him a large bundle of provisions. "Lest you turn to skin and bones during your travels," she said with a sad smile as she bid him farewell. His father, on the other hand, gave him four puppets to accompany him on his adventures.

The first figurine was a celestial being, a Burmese angel called Day Wa. The second was called Yo Kha, a giant who was legendary for his size and strength. The third puppet represented the well-known Saw Gyi—a magician in a red robe who wielded a white staff.

The last of the puppets was called Khe Ma. He was an old hermit in a simple robe with a bowl under his arm that he used when seeking alms.

Touched, Aung accepted the masterfully crafted marionettes and thanked his parents for all they had done for him. He then slung his pack, with the puppets fastened to the outside, up onto his back and set out on his journey.

Aung walked until evening fell and then paused under a banyan tree. Thinking it might be a good spot to rest for the night, he set down his pack to inspect the area. As he looked around, the figure of Day Wa, which dangled from his pack, caught his eye. Absentmindedly and almost without noticing that he had spoken the words aloud, Aung asked the puppet, "What do you think, Day Wa? Should I sleep here tonight?"

The last thing Aung expected was a response, yet seconds later he heard a voice answer: "I don't know, my dear Aung. I would look around carefully to make sure that it is safe here."

The young man stared wide-eyed at the wooden figure, which had now apparently begun to move and talk on its own. It was only the beginning of his journey. Was he already losing his mind? He looked over at the other puppets and saw that one after the other they, too, were coming to life! The giant Yo Kha pounded his fists together; the magician Saw Gyi stretched his stiff little body, and Khe Ma, the hermit, leaned back to gaze at the sunset.

Amazed by the mysteries of the universe, but dutifully following Day Wa's advice, Aung inspected the area he had chosen as his camp. It did not take him long to find tiger tracks! He was well and truly frightened and decided it would be best to spend the night high in the crown of the tree with his pack and puppets. Unable to sleep comfortably in his perch, he was awake in the middle of the night to see that two tigers did indeed appear beneath him to sniff and scratch at the tree trunk below. The next morning, Aung thanked his faithful puppets from the bottom of his heart for their sound guidance.

Aung continued on his way in good company through the mountains of Burma. Before long, in one of the mountain passes, he came upon a long caravan of rich traders. Aung was amazed by the treasures he saw as he beheld their many oxcarts piled high with valuable goods. He said to Yo Kha: "Why is the world so unfair? I wish more than anything that I could also have such riches!"

The likeness of the legendary giant nodded slowly. "Watch this," the puppet said, stomping his feet so fiercely that the ground began to tremble. The merchants looked around in alarm. An earthquake in the mountains could trigger landslides and falling rocks! When the shaking did not stop, a mortal terror overcame them. They jumped from their carts and ran, leaving their wares behind.

Once again overwhelmed, Aung rushed over to the abandoned carts. Was all of this now his? He ran his hands over the luxurious fabrics, tossed silver coins into the air, and hung a shining gold chain around his neck.

It was then that he heard the sound of sobbing from within the last wagon. Aung pulled back the tarp and there, looking up at him with angry, tear-stained eyes, was a young woman. It was Mala, the daughter of one of the merchants who had fled in panic. For Aung, it was love at first sight, but Mala, for her part, refused even to speak to him.

With his newly acquired riches, the young man built a large house for himself and his four marionettes, and he established a thriving business. His happiness would have been complete if only Mala had begun to speak to him. Though they lived under the very same roof, she refused to utter even one word and avoided Aung whenever possible. It seemed that she was simply waiting for the return of her father. Day Wa and Yo Kha advised him not to worry about the girl, but instead to concentrate on his business and increasing his wealth.

All the same, Aung tried very hard to win her favor. He gave her presents and pampered her with the most delicious food and drink. By this time, his riches had multiplied many times over, and he was convinced that Mala would at some point learn to be happy with her new life. At times he felt guilty about the way he had come by his fortune, but three of the puppets always reassured him. Only the hermit remained silent.

One day, during one of their many uncomfortably silent dinners, the leaden stillness was suddenly broken—Mala spoke! "I beg you: Give my father back his belongings. You now have much more than he ever did." No sooner did she speak these words than she immediately withdrew behind her curtain of impenetrable silence.

Aung consulted his puppets. He understood Mala well and was inclined to do as she asked, but Day Wa, Yo Kha, and Saw Gyi scoffed at him, calling him a fool and a weakling for entertaining such thoughts.

Before Aung had time to reach a decision, Mala received an unexpected visitor. Her father, who had long been searching, finally found her, and the two fled that same night. When Aung noticed the next morning that she had gone, he was overcome with grief and anger. He remained in his room and refused to speak to the three puppets he believed had served him so poorly. Eventually, the fourth puppet, Khe Ma the hermit, went in and sat down next to him. Although he had never paid much attention to Khe Ma, Aung now turned to him in desperation and begged him for guidance.

Khe Ma shook his head thoughtfully. For a long time he stared out the window in silence. Then he spoke: "My dear Aung, I own nothing save the bowl I use to collect alms. I have nothing to give you. But listen carefully, for what I tell you is true: I am content and happy, for I have everything I need."

Aung understood. The next morning, he went away, leaving behind the house and all of his possessions. He resolved to live from then on in solitude and to make do with whatever others were willing to share. In this way

Aung wandered from place to place until one day he came to a small, meager hut out of which a young woman emerged to give him food. Thankful for this kindness, he sank to his knees and waited, gaze averted, for her to fill his bowl. Then the woman spoke to him and the sound of her voice made him start. He looked up into her face and saw with surprise that the woman was Mala. With tears in his eyes, Aung revealed his identity and begged for forgiveness. Mala, impressed by his transformation but still wary, led him into the hut, where he fell to his knees before her father and apologized, begging his forgiveness as well. The father and his daughter forgave him and welcomed him with open arms into their home. They agreed to share equally everything they had.

The three set out and soon reached the large house. As he entered the yard, Aung spied the four puppets standing in the doorway. With a knowing smile they said: "So now you have found true happiness. Welcome home."

How the People of Bagan Started to Lie

Long ago the fabled city of Bagan in Myanmar was among the finest places in the world. The simple reason for its excellence was that its people did not lie. Regardless of how unpleasant it might sometimes be, they always told the truth and only the truth. According to legend, there was a device in the city with a mystical property: When a person who had lied in its presence held some part of his or her body in its opening, the device would slice that part off. With such an incentive close at hand, people lived together in harmony.

One day a woman called on a monk who also worked as a goldsmith and asked him kindly to fashion some gold that she owned into a ring. The monk willingly agreed, but as soon as she had left, he stashed the gold away with no intention of making anything from it.

A short time later the woman returned inquiring about the monk's progress, but the monk insisted that she had never given him any gold, that he had no idea what she was talking about.

The woman was flabbergasted. She had never experienced anything like it. Such a thing was unheard of in Bagan! She returned to the monk twice more, hoping each time to reason with him, but he would not be moved. It was unfathomable.

In the end the woman demanded that the monk go with her to the device to settle the matter once and for all. He agreed, asking her to wait one moment, during which he ran into his room to fetch the nugget of gold. Next he took his hollow bamboo walking stick, tucked the gold inside it, and sealed it up again. With the gold safely concealed in his staff, he set off with the woman and a handful of curious onlookers.

When they came to the device, the woman was the first to go. She put her hand into the opening and bitterly laid out her side of the story: She had trusted the scoundrel with her gold—a circumstance he flatly denied—and now he would not give it back to her.

No response from the device. It was plain for all to see that the woman was telling the truth. A murmur ran through the crowd, and people cast dim glances at the accused.

Now the monk stepped up to the device. Just a moment earlier he had turned to his adversary and requested that she hold his walking stick. To everyone's great astonishment he then put not his hand but his entire head into the machine and declared loudly and clearly: "I have already returned the gold to her, but she doesn't want to believe me." The assembled onlookers held their breath; surely the monk was lying.

But the machine did not stir. Pleased with himself, the monk rose and retrieved his walking stick. Looking down his nose at the woman, he then strode off. The stunned crowd eventually directed their disappointment and anger toward the device, pounding and tearing at it until nothing was left of it but scraps.

With the device destroyed, the era of truth in Bagan was at its end. In the absence of any mechanism to restrain it, dishonesty spread like an infectious disease.

The Sorrowbird

Once upon a time there was a young traveler named Khun San Lo. During a visit to a distant village he met a beautiful young woman named Nang Oo Pyin. The two fell in love and married. For some time they lived with the bride's parents and were very happy.

Eventually Khun San Lo asked his wife to return with him to his village, for he had not seen his mother in ages and missed her. Nang Oo Pyin agreed, and so they journeyed back to Khun San Lo's village, where his mother welcomed them both. Nang Oo Pyin became pregnant shortly thereafter. The overjoyed couple eagerly anticipated the birth of their first child.

Shortly before his wife's confinement Khun San Lo was compelled to travel on business. Promising to return as quickly as possible and certainly before the birth of their child, he left his bride in his mother's care.

Khun San Lo had hardly left the house when his mother revealed her true feelings. She was hopelessly jealous of Nang Oo Pyin and hated her from the bottom of her heart. In the days that followed she tormented her pregnant daughter-in-law in any way she could. She had Nang Oo Pyin doing all the housework, even scrubbing floors on her hands and knees. She would force the young woman to cook for her only to throw all of the food away. She found fault with everything Nang Oo Pyin did and required her to do everything twice. On many a night the exhausted young woman would cry herself to sleep.

When Nang Oo Pyin had had her fill of mistreatment she summoned all her courage and said to her mother-in-law: "I have done all that you ask, and still you torment me! Worse than that, you are endangering the life of my unborn child. I have no choice; I am going back to my own village to bring my child into the world."

Full of despair, Nang Oo Pyin set off on the arduous trek back home. Eventually the inevitable came to pass: Utterly drained and half-starved, she bore her child by the side of the road only to find, after all of her exertions, that her child had been stillborn.

Nang Oo Pyin wailed bitterly, disconsolate at the loss of both her child and her bright future. Her mother-in-law had robbed her of everything. She nestled her child in the branches of a nearby tree and dragged herself the rest of the way back home, where she tearfully recounted her misadventures and then died in her parents' arms.

In the meantime Khun San Lo had returned from his journey. At home he found only his overbearing mother, who reported how lazy and self-indulgent his bride had been; how she had soon left the house wishing never to hear from him again. "Forget her," was the embittered old woman's only advice.

Khun San Lo could not believe it. No, he thought. I love my dear wife; I must go to her. He set off without delay. But he was too late; Nang Oo Pyin had died just hours before his arrival in her village. At her deathbed her parents told him the truth, and he died beside his true love from grief and a broken heart.

The following day the greatest honor was to be bestowed on them: Their bodies would be burned on a funeral pyre. But Khun San Lo's mother had followed him, and when she saw him lying in state beside the hated daughter-in-law she ran straight up and laid a three-sectioned bamboo staff between the couple. Neither in death, nor even in their future lives would the two be united!

And so the souls of the couple live on among the stars in a constellation where two resplendent stars are separated by three fainter ones. As for the dead child, it transformed into a tiny bird that to this very day sings the most heart-wrenching of all birdsongs. The Burmese call it a sorrowbird.

Five Silver Coins

In a remote village there lived an old widow. Though very poor, she was pious and devout. She had no family, but everyone held her in high regard, not least of all because they could see her through a window in her hut each night kneeling before a little altar and praying for the entire village. By the light of a little oil lamp she would recite Buddhist scriptures, and she would end each night's ritual with the following refrain: "May all creatures live in health and peace."

One evening, however, the neighbors noticed that she had neither lit her lamp nor knelt before her altar. Her hut stood dark and quiet. Eventually they started to worry. Had some misfortune befallen the old woman?

A few of the neighbors eventually worked up the courage to go and inquire about her well-being. Night had already fallen when they knocked delicately at her door, asking: "Are you all right, ma'am?"

"I am fine," came the reply through the door. The villagers returned to their homes relieved but still confused.

On subsequent evenings it was just the same. No lamp was lit; no prayer was uttered. The villagers grew uneasy. What could have happened? Whyever was she neglecting the Buddha's teachings? Had she turned aside from the righteous path?

Some of the residents eventually returned to the old woman's house and told her quite openly what was troubling them: "We have grown so accustomed to your nightly recitation and prayers; it confuses and distresses us that you no longer seem so pious and devout."

The widow nodded thoughtfully. "I will explain everything. After my husband died I managed, through hard work, to set aside five precious silver coins. A few days ago a thief broke into my hut and stole those five coins. I am so dismayed that I can no longer pray." She shook her head sadly and bid her visitors a friendly but firm good night.

The news spread quickly, and it was not long before people decided something must be done to help the old woman. The villagers managed to scrape together five silver coins that they proudly presented to the widow.

The next night a small crowd gathered in front of her house to witness the resumption of the evening prayers. But still the hut was quiet and dark. After a while the villagers stormed up the steps, banged on the door, and demanded: "We've replaced your silver coins, ma'am! What's keeping you from your prayers?"

"Ah, children," replied the old woman, "it's true that thanks to your generosity I am once again in possession of five silver coins. But still I can find no peace of mind, for now I cannot help but think that if I had never been robbed, I would actually have ten silver coins!"

The Skylark's Revenge

Back when the Buddha still wandered the earth, there lived a little skylark. She had judiciously selected the most suitable grasses for her nest, favoring only the dry, faded blades that offered the best camouflage for her cushioned bower amid the tangled gray branches of undergrowth. When the nest was complete she laid her eggs gingerly, one after the other, taking especial care that their delicate shells did not touch. She kept a tireless watch and sheltered her clutch with her feathers, particularly during the sweltering heat of the day or when the wind swept across the grassland, threatening to dislodge the little nest.

A week or so later the skylark sensed that the chicks would soon hatch. A joyful occasion, yet the little bird worried. During the night she had heard a thunderous din in the distance. The ominous way it made her nest quiver had robbed her of all sleep. Soon enough it became clear that the mother bird's fears were completely justified, for the source of the disturbance was drawing closer. It was not long before a gigantic cloud of gray dust appeared some distance away. The clamor intensified, the dust cloud darkened, and the little bird realized that only a herd of elephants could cause such a tumult. And they were making straight for her nest.

Gathering all her courage, the little skylark scanned the area for a place where she might stop the herd before they reached her hedge. The little creature valiantly took up her post, determined to divert the oncoming beasts. The earth quaked beneath the mighty weight of the elephants, but the little skylark dug her claws into the dirt and stood her ground. As the contours of the first elephant emerged from the dust cloud she lifted her wings and bowed her head before him. She implored him to alter the path of the herd. The white leader was taken aback by this little bird who dared to pit herself against them, and he stopped to hear what she had to say. The skylark described her dire circumstance, how her delicate nest filled with eggs would be destroyed if the herd continued on their present course. Moved by the selfless courage of this tiny creature, the leader promised to give the nest and its contents a wide berth. But as he trod past he warned the skylark of the last elephant in the group, a wild and mutinous individual who would not be swayed by the leader. About this unruly beast's behavior the leader could make no promises.

As soon as the leader changed course, the other elephants followed his example. Every one of them took care to remain a suitable distance from the nest and its eggs. Only the last elephant disregarded the bird's request. Infuriated that such an insignificant creature would try in any way to influence an animal as large and majestic as himself, this headstrong pachyderm stubbornly followed his original course. When he reached the hedge where the nest lay, the gray monster purposefully trampled it, smashing all the eggs beneath his ponderous feet.

The skylark was grief-stricken at the loss of her nest and eggs. Her sorrow turned quickly to rage and a lust for revenge. Overcome with fury, the little bird swore to make the elephant pay. Her oath did not trouble the elephant in the least, however. He pointed out that there was little a skylark could do against his massive thick-skinned body, even if she managed to turn all the skylarks in the area against him. Amused by this thought, the elephant continued on his path of destruction, trampling heedlessly through the bush. This contempt only intensified the skylark's longing for vengeance, but a successful counterstrike called for a good strategy, so she summoned all of the animals of the bush to a council. Among the attendants were many close friends. When she reported what had happened there was unanimous agreement that such a cruel misdeed must be avenged.

It would be the crow's job to land on the giant animal and blind him by pecking out his eyes—the crow was justifiably feared for her razor-sharp beak. It would then be up to the fly to lay her eggs in the festering wounds; when the larvae hatched they would feed off the adjacent tissue so that the edges of the wounds would rankle and putrefy. As a result, the elephant would suffer fever and thirst. Then it would be the frog's turn. Since the blind elephant was likely to stumble about in search of some opportunity to quench his burning thirst, the frog would croak contentedly as if sitting on the bank of a cool river or stream. Unable to see and close to dying from thirst, the elephant would naturally assume that the croaking indicated a nearby water source and so follow the frog's voice. In reality, the frog would be drawing him to the edge of a cliff. At the critical moment the frog would fall silent, thus robbing the elephant of any frame of reference, without which the elephant would become desperate, take a step forward, and plummet into the abyss.

And that is just how it happened. The small animals set upon the evildoer as agreed, and soon the elephant was crashing blindly through the forest, feverish and parched, following the sound of a frog as a last desperate hope. He came to the edge of the chasm and stood there bewildered. All croaking had stopped. The frog hopped nimbly aside while the elephant took the fatal step and plunged off the cliff.

The rest of the herd had watched these events from a distance. Now the white leader stood before his followers and emphasized passionately how important it was to show respect for all living things, whether large or small. Even the smallest creature must be appreciated, for it, too, was a part of the whole. The frog, the fly, the crow, and the skylark could not have agreed more.

Saw Min Kyi and the Ruby

This is the story of Saw Min Kyi, a poor hardworking woman who lived with her mother in a little village a long time ago. She was in love with a stonemason who built houses and pagodas. The two loved each other very much, spent every free minute together, and hoped to marry one day.

Saw Min Kyi often went to the river with her mother to fish with their bamboo nets. One day it happened that a filthy stone drifted into Saw Min Kyi's net. She threw it back into the river, but a short time later it was again caught in her net. No matter how often she threw it into the water, it always reappeared. After a while mother and daughter took a break and wondered, might there be some deeper meaning behind this? And so they decided to take the stone home with them.

At the end of that long workday they returned to their hut, where Saw Min Kyi examined the stone more closely. She scrubbed away the encrusted filth, and how astonished the two women were when they saw what came to light: a big, red, shining ruby! It sparkled so brilliantly that the two women had no further need of lamps, and even their neighbors could see the light from afar.

News of this fabulous discovery traveled quickly, and soon the king himself caught wind of it. He decided to investigate the story of the marvelous gem for himself. He set out with his entire retinue, which caused quite a stir in Saw Min Kyi's tiny village. When the king had found Saw Min Kyi's house, the door opened, and the two inhabitants, full of humility, bowed deeply. They willingly showed the ruby to their ruler. Saw Min Kyi felt no attachment to it. Though it was beautiful, she had no practical use for it, and so she handed the gem over to the king, who put it directly into his treasury.

A short time later, when the king desired to examine the precious object at leisure, he found that it was no longer in the treasury. The stone had inexplicably returned to Saw Min Kyi, who had once again found it in her net while fishing.

When the king learned of this, he commanded that Saw Min Kyi be brought to the castle, and he married her. From then on the queen led a life of sufficient opulence to make even the ladies of the court pale with envy.

Alas, Saw Min Kyi herself was unhappy. She missed her mother, and above all she missed her dear stonemason. She contemplated in sorrow how she might change her situation. Then it occurred to her to have a pagoda built with her magnificent ruby. As everyone knows, erecting a pagoda builds good karma. Perhaps she and her beloved, those intertwined but separated souls, might then have better luck in their next lives? The king consented, and Saw Min Kyi arranged for the work to begin. Moved by her desire, she enlisted her beloved stonemason as the builder. He began immediately to execute the plans.

As it happened, Saw Min Kyi's position and the preferential treatment she enjoyed from the king were sources of envy and jealousy among the ladies of the court. They soon learned that the stonemason for the new pagoda was the queen's former lover, and a deceitful rumor made the rounds that Saw Min Kyi had beguiled the king and would now betray him with her old flame.

When this news was brought to the king he was beside himself with rage. Without further ado he had Saw Min Kyi, his queen, detained and interrogated. He wished to know whether it was true that she had once loved the stonemason. She admitted it was, but insisted that she had never been unfaithful to her husband. He refused to believe her and sentenced her to death. Saw Min Kyi accepted all of this with grace and composure. She had only one request: that her dead body be thrown into the nearby river; and she prophesied that if the accusations were true and she was guilty, her body would drift downstream, as expected. But if she was innocent, her body would slowly drift against the current.

The king scoffed at such a fanciful notion but promised to honor her wish. Early the next morning Saw Min Kyi was put to death. Two executioners pressed a thick bamboo staff against her throat and threw her body into the river. The people—and secretly the king—then watched intently to see what would happen with the body.

At first Saw Min Kyi's corpse did not move at all. Ever so slowly, however, after a seeming eternity, it began to drift...upstream.

Seeing this, the king was so smitten with grief and remorse that he fell dead on the spot. To this day, we are told, one can still visit the Saw Min Kyi pagoda in the old capital Mrauk U in Rakhine State. In its spire is set the legendary ruby. There is a place on the banks of a nearby river where no grass will grow, and the Rakhine people say that it was here that Saw Min Kyi was unjustly put to death.

The Night the Moon Fell into the Well

There once lived a simple farmer who kept his opinions to himself and never bothered anyone. He was, however, not known for being the sharpest tool in the shed. People called him a simpleton, an empty-headed fool, and truth be told, they were right.

One night, the farmer awoke and was thirsty. He went out to draw a bucket of water from the well. The night was clear and the moon shone brightly in the sky as he plodded across the yard. He did not notice the moon up above, but as he looked down into the well, there in the water he saw the reflection of the bright orb shining brilliantly back up at him. He was shocked! What was the moon doing all the way down in the well? How in the world did it get there?

He just had to rescue the moon, he thought, but how? Glancing around, he spied the rope with its metal hook at one end, which he usually used to hoist the water bucket. Full of zeal, he tossed it into the well and let it sink to the bottom.

No sooner did the hook break the surface of the water than it caught on a stone. The farmer pulled and pulled on the rope but it did not budge. The moon is truly very heavy, the fatigued man thought, and then pulled once more with all his might. Suddenly, the hook freed itself and shot back up out of the well. The momentum was so great that the farmer fell over backwards while the hook sailed over him in a great arc.

Lying there in the dirt, the farmer now saw the moon overhead—shining, white, and very large. You could not miss it. He was astonished. All by himself, by his strength alone, he had pulled the moon out of the well and back up into the sky! Worn out, but very proud and deeply satisfied, the farmer went back to his room and returned to his bed. His thirst was already long forgotten.

Little Monkey Goes Looking for Trouble

Mother monkey lived with her children deep in the jungle in Burma. Each morning, she set out to search for food and warned her young ones not to climb down from the tree alone while she was gone or else they would be in deep trouble.

The little monkeys promised to wait for her and sat patiently all day until she returned with food.

One day, the youngest, a little boy monkey named Maung Nyho, asked his older siblings if they knew what this "trouble" even was.

They had no idea.

"Is it dangerous?"

The siblings had no answer.

"Does it make us sick?"

The other children were completely stumped and told him to hush up.

"Well if you don't know what it is, then I am going to go find out," said the youngest monkey, and in one giant leap he sprang down from the tree.

"Where do you think you are going?" cried his brothers and sisters. "Get back here!" But Maung Nyho was already gone.

All alone, he ran through the jungle looking for trouble.

Suddenly, a deer bounded past him, running for his life from the hungry lion that was chasing it.

"Hold on a minute," the little monkey called after him. "Can you tell me what trouble is?"

"Trust me! You really don't want to know," the deer called back and kept on running.

After a while, Maung Nyho came upon two boys who were trying to light a small campfire. The monkey climbed up a tree to watch. The wood the boys were using was wet and as much as they tried they could not get it to burn.

"This is too much trouble," said one of the boys to the other.

The monkey did not understand what sticks and twigs could possibly have to do with trouble. Disappointed, he climbed down from the tree and crept away.

Eventually he came upon a dwarf's hut. Maung Nyho knocked on the door. From within he heard a voice: "Who is it? What do you want?"

"I am a monkey child and want to know what trouble is."

The dwarf opened the door. "You really want to find out what it is, huh?"

"Yes."

"Then take this crate," answered the dwarf, pointing to a wooden box that lay on the floor. "Drag it to a meadow on the edge of the forest and open it. Then you will know what trouble is."

Maung Nyho did as he was told. He pulled the crate through the jungle until he reached a large clearing and set it down exactly in the middle. Slowly he opened the lid. Out sprang a huge, aggressive dog, and the little monkey ran for his life. There were no trees to climb in the clearing and the forest was far away. He screamed for help at the top of his lungs but no one rushed to save him. The dog was getting closer and closer but at the last second, the monkey reached the forest and jumped up into a tree. Below him sat the snarling dog. The little monkey called plaintively for his mother. Hearing the cries of her youngest child, she hurried to him.

"Please forgive me, Mother," said the little one. "Now I know what trouble is and from now on I will always listen to you."

The Farmer's Revenge

Long ago there lived in Burma a merchant who frequently traveled. He wandered from village to village, mostly in the mountains, buying and selling at the markets. On one of these expeditions he contracted a terrible case of malaria. A friendly farmer took him in and tended to him in his own bed. The merchant spent several days in a twilit delirium before the farmer and his family were finally able to nurse him back to health. When he had fully recovered and was taking leave of his newfound friends, he warmly encouraged the farmer to visit him in his village on the Irrawaddy River. It would be his privilege, nay, his duty, to welcome this man as an honored guest in his home. After all, the farmer had saved his life!

The following summer the farmer decided to visit the merchant. It was not an easy journey, but the farmer rode his best and dearest horse. Slowly they made their way down out of the mountains onto the wide plain and from there swiftly on to the merchant's house.

"My savior, my friend, my brother, all that I have is yours. Stay as long as you like!" cried the overjoyed merchant at their reunion.

The farmer was introduced around the village, and the neighbors took such a liking to him that he had to spend most of his time visiting new acquaintances and keeping up with all the villagers' invitations. They would drink tea, chat about this and that, and invariably the stranger would be treated to a delicious meal.

After a few days, however, it appeared that the host was disappointed by his guest's frequent absences. "You're spending all your time with the neighbors," he gently rebuked the farmer. "I'm feeling a bit neglected, and I wonder if I might borrow your grand horse to go visit my relatives in the neighboring villages. Will you lend it to me for a few days?"

Without hesitation the farmer permitted his friend to use his horse. Impatient and rash, the merchant rode the horse for three days from sunrise till sunset so that in the end it returned drained, weakened, and of little further use to the famer.

The farmer, meanwhile, had been enjoying himself immensely among his new friends, and he was bitterly enraged by the careless mishandling of his favorite horse. He swore to get revenge. With suppressed rage and a feigned smile he asked to borrow the merchant's boat. Permission was granted, and the farmer marched grimly to the dock. "Since he abused my horse, I will abuse his boat," he grumbled.

For three days from sunrise till sunset the farmer rowed the boat hither and yon on the Irrawaddy. But at the end of that time the sturdy wooden boat showed nary a sign of wear while the farmer's hands were riddled with blisters, not to mention how swollen they were!

Revenge had utterly lost its appeal. The farmer bid his host a hasty farewell and set off on the long journey home holding the reins of his enfeebled horse, who now barely managed to plod along beside him.

The Fisherman and His Wife

There was once a young but very poor fisherman who lived in a village by the sea. He longed to find a wife, but the search was proving exceedingly difficult. None of the desirable young women wanted the poor fisherman for a husband. After a long time, he finally found himself a bride who, though not the most beautiful, was the cleverest in the village.

The first time the two of them went down to fish together, the young man saw a crow sitting atop a stupa. "Look at that crow!" he cried. "How white it is!"

"Indeed," replied his wife. "It is truly astonishingly white."

The two reached the beach, where a gull stood in the sand.

"Look at that gull!" the man called anew. "How black its plumage!"

"Indeed," replied his wife. "It is truly astonishingly black."

They went out to sea, and although the work was arduous and wearisome, they dispatched it with ease and returned with a net full of fish.

From that day on the couple always fished together, and they worked in such harmony that they soon became wealthy.

Their good fortune did not go unnoticed, and one day a neighbor decided to follow them with his own wife and to copy everything they did.

As this other couple passed the stupa on their way down to the sea, they saw the crow perched upon it, and the man cried: "There's a crow. It's completely white."

"It's black," contradicted his wife.

A little later they came to the beach, where a gull was strutting across the sand.

"A black gull," the man said. "Have you ever seen anything like it?"

"Are you blind? It's white, not black, you numbskull!"

The couple fell to quarreling and trading unkind words. They spent the whole day bickering until in the evening they returned to the village without a single fish.

The Pious Queen

Once there was a king and queen who loved each other very much and who lived happily together in their palace. It was the king's greatest pleasure to spend the entire day with his wife. The queen, however, divided her devotion between her husband and the teachings of the Buddha. In fact, she was unable to find sufficient time in her daily routine to meditate and to study the scriptures, so she asked her husband for permission to spend four weeks living modestly with nothing to distract her from the words of the Enlightened One.

The king cared so much for his wife that he consented, albeit with a heavy heart, and not without asking her to arrange in advance for some suitable companionship during her absence.

And so the queen undertook to find for her husband a woman who would attend to him for a month. She sent forth the ladies of the court, who soon returned with a suitable young woman who was more than delighted when she learned what was asked of her.

For the next month, life in the royal palace played out thus: The king and his attendant occupied the upper story, where by all accounts she tended to him well and lovingly. The queen, meanwhile, lived on the lower floor, cleaning and cooking, showing generosity to the monks on their thrice-daily alms rounds, meditating, reading Buddhist scriptures, and attending sermons at nearby monasteries.

As the month drew to a close, however, the king's young attendant felt disinclined to depart. During those weeks she had grown quite accustomed to the luxurious palace life. Faced with the prospect of leaving the king and the grand house, her mind turned to wicked thoughts, and she devised a scheme to do away with her rival.

One morning, knowing the queen's daily routines, she prepared a pot of boiling oil. From a staircase high above she then took aim at her adversary, who was busily sweeping the landing below. At the critical moment, however, the queen moved forward in order to clean the next step, and the oil splashed behind her on the floor. The queen looked serenely up at the young woman while a servant raced up the stairs with a loud cry and tore furiously at the attacker's hair.

To the astonishment of everyone present, the queen broke up this tussle, and even pacified the king, who was beside himself with rage when he heard the news. The queen calmly led the young woman into the courtyard and even sent her off with something to eat and a bit of gold.

The young woman slunk away in tears, head bowed in shame.

Nan Kyar Hae and the Guardian Spirit

There was once a beautiful young villager named Nan Kyar Hae whose charm attracted the attention of King Theikthadharma Thiriraza. She had traveled with her parents from their small village to a place near the palace to help construct a new pagoda, and when the king laid eyes on her, he burned with love for her and resolved to make her his queen. Nan Kyar Hae's mother and father were overjoyed that fortune had smiled upon their daughter. Now, the king had only recently assumed the throne, thus in addition to the completion of a shrine there were many other duties to be attended to, so the wedding ceremony was arranged in great haste. They were so pressed for time that the young woman's family completely forgot to ask the village's guardian spirit to bless the marriage, as was the custom in their small community. The villagers warned the bride and her parents against spurning the *nat* in this manner, but their concerns fell on deaf ears.

After the wedding, the king, who was unaware that a custom had been broken, led his wife home. Life in the extravagant castle, though it offered every imaginable comfort, brought the new queen no joy. She fell ill, and her condition worsened with each passing day. The king's personal doctors did their utmost to restore the queen's health but every effort proved futile.

Eventually the king summoned a fortune-teller, who explained that the illness was the work of the *nat* from the queen's village. He explained that the spirit was resentful because he had not been asked to bless the marriage. In order to appease him, the queen's mother and father were called to the palace to take their daughter back to their village to perform the task they had neglected. The illness was too advanced, however, and their belated attempt at reparations was to no avail: When the family arrived in the village, the spirit transformed into a tiger and rushed at the failing young queen, who died instantly of a heart attack.

A Battle Between Two Sculptors

In a monastery in a Burmese village there lived a big-hearted abbot who was admired and beloved by all. Not long before his eightieth birthday, the villagers pooled together a significant sum of money in order to build a pagoda in the abbot's honor and dedicate it to him on his birthday.

Construction progressed quickly and the work was done with weeks to spare. Only then did the crestfallen villagers realize that they did not have enough money to commission the obligatory statue of the Buddha for the main altar. It occurred to them, however, that two particularly pious monks from their very own monastery were also talented sculptors. One of them worked primarily in stone, the other in wood. The villagers approached the monks and asked them for help. "We don't know yet whether it should be a stone or wooden statue," they said. "Would you each be willing to make one so that we can decide?"

The monks agreed, and side by side they started to chisel. After a few days the pieces began to take shape, and the villagers came in growing numbers to view the work and to offer their opinions on which of the two figures should occupy the place of honor in the pagoda. Almost from the start there were two parties embroiled in a boisterous debate, and soon enough the monks found themselves swept along by the spirit of competition and rivalry. They glared at one another and labored to exhaustion on their pieces.

When they were finished, the two artists anxiously presented their work. The crowd was amazed, for both of the works were truly extraordinary. Yet even now that they were complete, the villagers could not agree on which to choose. Arguments and scuffles broke out.

"This is all your fault!" one of the monks shouted. "This is an outrage!" growled the other in reply, and it quickly came to blows between them. They beat one another with their bare fists, but their anger grew, fanned by the rowdy mob, until they began striking one another with their completed masterpieces. When the dust finally settled, the two monks lay dead on the floor, their skulls staved in, broken Buddhas in their hands.

The Village of Endless Sermons

In the northern region of Burma was a mountain village with a dubious reputation: The villagers were all so pious that they demanded especially long sermons. The monks were expected to preach for hours and hours!

This was hard on the monks, since the villagers refused to give alms or food to those who did not live up to their expectations. Many of the monks simply left. The length of the sermons so adversely affected the health of those who tried to stay that they, too, eventually fled out of fear for their lives. Consequently the village monastery was soon completely uninhabited. "The Village of Endless Sermons" it was called, and everyone steered clear of it.

At long last, to the delighted surprise of the villagers, a monk finally came to them. He was short and stout, and as they would soon discover, he ate astonishing amounts of food. The monk defended himself saying, "If you want to hear my sermon, I must have my strength, and to be strong I need fortification!"

The new monk seemed very knowledgeable, devout, and learned, however, and so the village provided him with everything he desired and eagerly awaited his first sermon, which was set to be held on the day of the next full moon. As no one else was available to fill the position, they even made him the abbot of their monastery.

The day of the full moon came and at midday the entire village assembled at the monastery—even the children were present. The abbot rose and began his sermon. An hour passed, yet each and every member of the audience sat still as a mouse and listened attentively. Another hour passed and not even any of the children had made a peep. After four hours, however, a few of the children began to yawn, and after five hours the women slowly stole out of the room, taking the children with them. The monk kept on talking. More hours passed, the sun went down, and one after another the men slipped away. When the first cock crowed only the village elder remained before the abbot, who still gave no sign of quitting. The old man, almost overpowered by sleep, tried to creep backwards away from the monk toward the door through which he hoped to escape this torture. But to his horror he realized that the monk was following him step for step into the courtyard. The elder stood up and ran but he failed to see the well and tumbled head over heels into it.

Luckily the well was not very deep and the elder was not seriously hurt, but now he was trapped in the cold water at the bottom. Above him stood the abbot, carrying steadfastly on with his litany. After an hour of this, compassion overcame the monk and he asked the man in the well, "Shall I continue until the sun is up, or have you had enough?"

The miserably freezing village elder said weakly: "That was enough, Your Holiness. I can assure you that our village will never again demand long sermons from our monks."

The Long Journey

In the Irrawaddy delta lived a young rice farmer with his mother and father. He was industrious, honest, and well-liked by everyone who knew him. One morning he did not feel well. His mother cooked him a strong curry to pep him up, but his discomfort persisted. The next day he felt so poorly that he could not even go out to work his field. By the third day, he was unable to leave the hut. His mother sought the village healer's help, but his herbs, salves, and teas offered no relief.

The concerned father hurried to other nearby villages and asked their healers and women for help, but none of their advice had any effect; the young farmer's condition worsened by the day. When the local astrologer heard of this, he went to the family and consulted the stars for them. His horoscope revealed that in a kingdom far to the east, there lived a famous astrologer who could help the ailing farmer.

The mother and father were sure that such a long journey would be too much for their son and begged him not to go, but fearing he would die if he stayed in the village, the young man set out on his way.

At the end of his first day of travel he reached a banyan tree under which he set up camp for the night. No sooner had he lain down than the *nat* appeared, the tree's guardian spirit.

"Where are you headed, traveler?" he asked curiously.

"I am journeying to seek a famous astrologer."

"An astrologer!" cried the spirit joyfully. "Could you please do me a favor?"

"It would be my pleasure," the young man replied. "How can I help you?"

"I have been living in this old tree now for so long, and I would very much like to go somewhere else. But whatever I do, I can't manage to leave it. Can you please ask the astrologer why I am bound to this tree?"

"I would be glad to," he promised, tired from the arduous trek.

The next day he started out before the sun was even in the sky. After a few hours he came to a small hill, at the foot of which lay a large snake.

"Where are you headed, traveler?" she asked.

"I am journeying to seek a famous astrologer."

"An astrologer!" the snake cried with glee. "Will you please ask him for me why it is that I can't leave this accursed hill no matter how hard I try?"

"It would be my pleasure," replied the sick young man. "I will come by on my way back and give you his answer."

On he traveled until he came to a wide, raging river. He searched for a bridge or a ferry but found no way across. Exhausted, he sank to his knees in the sand at the river's edge. Was this the end of the road? Would he ever get well again?

All of a sudden a crocodile swam up to him. "Where are you headed, traveler?" he asked curiously.

"I am journeying to seek a famous astrologer," the young man replied in a despondent voice. "But I am afraid that my journey ends here; I cannot swim a river with such a strong current."

"An astrologer!" cried the crocodile happily. "Don't worry about the river. I will bring you to the other side, but you must first promise me something."

"Whatever you want."

"Please ask him why I can't dive underwater. I am a crocodile, after all!"

"I'll ask him for you. I promise."

The reptile slid to the edge of the river, the young man clambered onto his back, and the crocodile delivered him safely to the opposite shore.

Still weak from his illness but in good spirits, he continued on his way. After many hours he reached a kingdom at the borders of which were posted signs warning strangers not to enter. Trespassers faced the death penalty. The young man had no other choice, however, and so he walked on. It was not long before a palace guard discovered him, arrested him, and brought him before the king.

"How dare you enter my realm!" cried the monarch angrily. "Are you not aware that the punishment for this is death?"

"I am sorry," replied the fearful young man in a weak voice. "What was I supposed to do? I am journeying to seek a famous astrologer and the path to him leads right through your kingdom. I humbly beg your forgiveness."

The king was on the verge of answering that he knew no mercy and that the intruder was to be executed at dawn when the soft voice of the princess rang through the room. "Stranger, you say that you are on your way to a famous astrologer. Please ask him for me what my future holds." The king could not believe his ears. Since her birth his daughter had not spoken a word, and all believed her to be deaf and dumb. Could he really condemn the man to whom his daughter had spoken her first words? And who would ask the astrologer about the princess if the foreigner's journey ended here? He decided to pardon the young man on the condition that he return to the castle to relay the stargazer's prophecy.

Relieved, the young man promised to do just that and continued on his way.

After a long journey he finally reached the hut of the famed astrologer. In front of the hut waited a long line of people who, like him, had traveled great distances. Patiently, the weary young man waited for his turn.

Inside the hut, amid candles, books, and papers, there sat an old man. The mere sight of him evoked such reverence in the sick man that he scarcely dared open his mouth.

"I am very sick," he finally explained quietly. "My parents have tried to nurse me back to health. They cared for me and called on every healer they could find, but no one could help me. This is why I would like to know my future. Am I to die soon?"

For a long time the astrologer said nothing. At last he replied, "If you had not undertaken the journey to see me, then you would indeed have died. Now that you have accomplished that feat, you will also manage to get over your illness. You will become a rich and happy man."

Relieved and elated, the young man thanked him. He already felt somewhat better and wanted to rise when he suddenly remembered his promises. But should he really take up even more of the astrologer's precious time? Did he not already have the information he sought? He hesitated. "Honored master," he ventured after a long pause, "May I ask something else in the name of all the friends I met along my way?"

The astrologer nodded.

"The daughter of the king whose kingdom I crossed is already sixteen years old yet does not speak a word. Will this ever change?"

"Oh!" laughed the old and wise man. "That is an easy question. The king must allow his daughter to marry the first man to whom she speaks. From then on she will have no trouble speaking."

"On the way I met a crocodile who asked me to seek your advice because he cannot dive under the water."

"For that, too, there is a solution," the astrologer replied. "There is a magical stone stuck in its head. Once that stone is removed, the animal will be able to swim under the water."

The young man felt the exhaustion from his long journey throughout his whole body, and he wanted nothing more than to lie down and rest, but there were two more promises he did not want to break. And so he told about the snake and asked for advice on her behalf.

"She does not know this, but she is guarding a large ruby. The gem is hidden under the hill. Dig it up and she will be able to slither away wherever she pleases."

Lastly, the young man told of the *nat* in the banyan tree.

The astrologer had a solution for this problem, too. "Under the tree lies a pot of gold that the spirit is protecting. As soon as the gold is excavated, the spirit may go free."

The thankful young man took his leave and gathered his strength for the long and difficult journey back. After a few days, as the astrologer had predicted, he felt a bit better and set out on his way.

His long return journey finally brought him to the palace, where the king could barely contain his excitement. "Tell me then, traveler, what did the astrologer say?"

The young man repeated the recommendation word for word.

Recalling that his daughter's first words had been to the stranger and trusting in the power of the stars, the king granted the stranger his daughter's hand in marriage. From then on she spoke and conversed as if there had never been a problem.

Her husband, now a prince, wanted to take his bride with him to his village in order to introduce her to his mother and father, and the two began their long journey the very next day.

That evening they reached the large river, where they found the unhappy crocodile lying on the bank watching the others dive below the surface.

"Did you keep your word and ask the astrologer about me?" he wanted to know immediately.

"Of course," replied the young man, who was now feeling fit as a fiddle. He recounted the astrologer's words. The crocodile had, in fact, always noticed a certain pressure under his scalp and when the princess inspected the area closely, she found a slight bump. Using a small knife, she made a little incision over the bump and out fell a large gem that sparkled brilliantly when it caught the sun's light.

Out of gratitude, the crocodile transported the two to the opposite side of the river and gave the precious stone to the prince. He was so pleased that he also told them about a shortcut they could take on the way back to their village. The prince was not interested in this advice, however, as he was still beholden to two other friends.

The prince and princess trekked on until they met the snake, still sadly slithering around her hill. The prince relayed the astrologer's wisdom, and with the snake's permission, they began to dig. After a short while, they found a ruby so large, even the princess had never seen the like of it at her father's court. The snake felt a great relief and knew that she was now free. "Keep the ruby!" she called to them as she disappeared into the bushes, never to be seen again.

At last they reached the banyan tree. The prince went up close to the trunk and told the tree what he had heard from the astrologer. For a long time he heard nothing except for the rustling of the leaves in the wind.

"The pot of gold," came the spirit's voice suddenly, "is under the roots that point to the west. Dig it up and take it so that I can finally be free."

The prince and princess did as they were told and traveled on until they reached the village. From that day forward, the young man remained not only healthy, but also wealthy and happy in the companionship of his wife.

On Gratitude

When the Buddha still lived and wandered the world spreading his teachings, he had a student named Ananda, a man filled with gratitude, generosity, and serenity. Together they traveled to an unknown region where the Buddha sent Ananda ahead to the palace to meet with the king. The king was extremely wealthy, and as it happened, Ananda arrived at the palace just as a shipment of a thousand robes arrived from abroad. The king immediately distributed half of these luxurious garments among his many wives.

It was not long before many of the palace residents, including the king's wives, showed great interest in what Ananda had to say. To pay him homage, they gave him their robes and declared their intentions to live more in accordance with his teachings. A short time later the king threw a grand party and bade his wives wear their new robes. They were unable to comply with his request, however, because they had already given their costly robes to Ananda!

When the king learned of this he was furious with the preacher, who had not only been living under his roof, but had also enriched himself at the king's expense. He called Ananda before him in order to take him to task.

"I have heard that the Buddha requires modesty and that one should own no more than three robes for daily use," he cried angrily. "Yet you have accepted five hundred robes as presents!"

Ananda smiled. "You are right," he answered. "But my master does not say how many donations we are allowed to receive." He led the king to his simple quarters. "The robe is used first as an outer garment and later as an undergarment once it begins to wear," he explained. "Next we use it for bedding and then as a rug," Ananda continued. "When it becomes too filthy even for that we can always use it to wipe our feet when we come inside. Finally, we tear the cloth into strips, mix those with clay, and then use the material to build walls." The king was deeply impressed and gave all the remaining robes to Ananda, the Buddha, and his followers.

Ananda then gave one of these robes to a student as a symbol of his gratitude for the student's help with his daily chores, including the cooking and cleaning. In turn, this student selflessly passed the robe along to a friend. The costly garment drew the attention of the Buddha's followers, who became upset and complained to the Buddha that Ananda clearly favored certain individuals who had now amassed such great riches that they were giving precious goods away.

A smile flashed over the Buddha's face. Ananda had simply understood the deeper meaning of gratitude and respect, he explained.

In order to illustrate the meaning of gratitude and modesty, he told the following story:

There was once a lion that lived with his family on top of a mountain surrounded by a forest and various rivers and lakes. Around the mountain lived Cat, Hare, Deer, and Fox. Hare and Deer were grazing peacefully by one of the rivers when Lion, on a hunt, sprang down from the mountain with a mighty leap. The other animals fled in fear, but the lion soon realized that his paws were stuck in the mud he had landed in. The hot sun rapidly dried the wet earth and now Lion was trapped.

For seven days, Lion languished there until he was starving and weak. At last he saw Fox passing by in the distance.

"Fox, help me! I'm stuck!" cried Lion desperately.

Reluctantly, Fox came nearer. "If I free you," he said hesitantly, "how do I know that you won't eat me?"

"No, no, I would never do that," promised the lion, gasping for breath. "I am terribly exhausted; I can hardly stay on my feet. Oh please! Save me! I would be forever grateful!"

Fox decided to help and started digging away at the dirt around the lion's paws. He was able to soften the mud with water, and in the end he pulled the lion free.

Lion proved his gratitude by killing a buffalo for Fox, and even though it went against his nature, he also held back and waited until Fox had eaten his fill before helping himself to the leftovers. Finally, taking a large piece of meat in his jaws, Fox prepared to take his leave.

Lion, however, still felt deeply indebted to Fox and proposed the following: Would Fox perhaps like to come live with the lions in their spacious cave on top of the mountain where there was always enough to eat? Fox accepted the offer, and starting the very next day, the two families lived together in the great cave, sharing all their food and hunting together.

After a while the lioness started to feel that Lion was paying more attention to the foxes than to his own sons. She said to the vixen: "You all have lived with us for quite some time now. It's getting a little cramped, don't you think? Wouldn't it be nice to be back in your own den?" The young lions made similar comments, and the foxes, sensing that they were no longer welcome, prepared to move out. Before they left, however, Fox wanted to hear what the father lion thought about the matter.

When Lion heard what had happened he was indignant. He gathered his family together and explained insistently: "I lay there dying of thirst in the sun when Fox, in spite of the danger to himself, saved my life. Every one of us is greatly indebted to him, and we must all be thankful. Besides, when has there ever been a time limit on gratitude?"

The lioness and the children nodded. They understood, and from then on the lion and fox families lived peacefully together in the cave.

The Traveling Threesome

A father and his son wanted to go on a journey, so the father sent the son to the barn to fetch the donkey to carry their packs. When the donkey had been laden, they felt sorry for the poor animal on account of its heavy load, so they decided not to ride on it but to walk beside it.

They set off and soon came to the first village. Immediately they noticed the stares of the villagers. Why weren't they riding their donkey, the villagers scoffed. What a waste! When the father and son heard this, they decided that the son should ride the donkey, because, after all, the people had a point.

They traveled on in this manner and soon reached the next village. This time the villagers were downright angry—how disrespectful it was for the son to not let his father ride the donkey but to hog it for himself! Naturally, the son did not want to appear disrespectful, so he quickly jumped down and helped his father up into the saddle.

Hoping that they had now done everything right, the two continued on their way. The path rose to a steep incline and while the father was able to ride in comfort, the son began to sweat profusely beside him. On top of the mountain they discovered a small settlement, and the son rushed into it for a drink of water. When the locals came out of their huts to greet the visitors, they were appalled to see the son so exhausted while the father was still fit as a fiddle. What kind of a terrible, selfish father was this? They told him to get out and never come back.

Confused, the father and son stood at the edge of the village. They only had one option left, so they both mounted the brave little donkey.

After a while they reached another village. As the father and his son rode through on their panting pack animal, the villagers stared at them. Two people riding on this poor, abused, half-dead donkey! What shameful behavior! What kind of coldhearted brutal individuals these strangers must be!

Immediately, father and son dismounted and left the village as quickly as they could. As soon as they were out of sight, they stopped to catch their breath. After a while the son turned to his father and asked, perplexed: "So now what do we do?"

How the Hare Became a Judge

Once there were two farmers living in a small village where the calving season had just begun. One of the two neighbors was known for his cleverness. He owned a cow that was on the verge of giving birth. The other neighbor, generally regarded as a bit simple, owned a horse that was about to foal, and he was very pleased because on a farm horses had great value as work animals.

One night after both of the neighbors had gone to bed, the clever farmer's cow and the simple farmer's mare both went into labor.

Now it was widely known that the clever farmer suffered from insomnia. He rarely slept soundly, so he woke the minute the noise began. Hearing both the pitiful lowing of the calf and the vigorous whinnies of the foal, he correctly concluded that both his cow and his neighbor's mare had brought their offspring into the world.

It being still the middle of the night with the moon barely visible in the sky, the scheming neighbor lit a torch and hurried along the path to the place where the animals were kept. He went first to his cow's stable and checked on the healthy little calf by the light of the torch. He saw no light in the nearby stall where the horse was stabled and supposed that his neighbor, a deep sleeper, had not been woken by the din, so he decided to take a quick look for himself. He could make out the contours of a handsome colt lying peacefully in the straw. Since there was no sign of his neighbor, the sly farmer decided to seize this golden opportunity. He returned to his own stable, took the calf in his arms, and carried it to the neighbor's stable, where he laid it snugly beside the mare. Then he took the colt and carried it to his own stable, where he left it in the care of the cow. Satisfied with this deceit, he returned to his bed to rest a few more hours.

He knew, however, that news of the unusual birth needed to make the rounds before his simple neighbor had a chance to put two and two together. And so despite his lack of sleep, the clever farmer was out and about very early telling everyone he met in the village of the miraculous incident in his stable. Many incredulous villagers put aside their morning chores to get a glimpse of the cow that had borne a foal. As the sly neighbor had anticipated, these villagers were then willing to testify to the marvelous event. Right there in the humble thatched shelter there truly was a big cow with a little foal nestled into the warm coat of her heavy body. The awestruck villagers beheld the animals in amazement, but their reverent silence was abruptly shattered when the simple farmer arrived to accuse the clever farmer of having stolen his foal.

The sly farmer tried to ease tempers by explaining to his simple neighbor that it must just be a quirk of nature that a cow brought a foal into the world. Not persuaded in the least, the simple neighbor objected that the story would be more credible if a calf had not been found beside a mare the very same morning. It was not a case of some extraordinary miracle, but rather an underhanded swap of the two newborn animals. The conniving neighbor tried to paint it all as remarkable coincidence: two unnatural events that just happened to occur on the same night. This explanation in no way convinced the simple neighbor, and so he called on the villagers to help him win back the foal that was rightfully his.

The villagers had no idea what to do. None of them knew the details of what had transpired, so it was just one neighbor's word against the other's, and they were hesitant to take sides. They told the two farmers they would have to find some other means of settling their dispute. Since the villagers were clearly unwilling to get involved, the simple neighbor decided to seek the help of an outsider to mediate the absurd situation. Unfortunately their village was so small that there were no higher authorities one could turn to in cases like this. The owner of the horse therefore insisted that the owner of the cow go with him to the neighboring village to find an impartial judge. They set out at once.

On the way the two farmers met a hare, and because they knew that hares had the reputation of being just, they asked if he would be willing to arbitrate for them. The hare asked them to lay out the details of the case, and after listening carefully he agreed to resolve the matter for them. Apparently the hare was widely known and much in demand in these parts, however. He told them that he had no time to devote to the case today, but that he would be willing to meet again with both parties in a week's time. The official hearing would take place in their village. Furthermore, all evidence and all witnesses in the case must be present or readily available. Above all, the session must start promptly, first thing in the morning, as soon as the sun appeared on the horizon.

It was an unaccustomed honor to welcome such an esteemed and erudite judge to the village. When the much-anticipated day of the hearing arrived and the first fiery sunbeams were just touching the fields, nearly all of the village's inhabitants turned out to see for themselves what light the hare meant to shed on the confusing case of the mismatched farm animals. The prolonged conflict had divided the community and disturbed the idyllic peace that normally reigned in the village. The inhabitants hoped that the hare's ruling might serve to restore the calm and the introspective quiet they had previously enjoyed. While they waited patiently, scanning the landscape for the first signs of their approaching guest, the early-morning sun began its leisurely ascent. The morning came and went in this fashion without any sign of the hare. Even during the midday hours, when the sun burned mercilessly down on them, the villagers bore the blazing, murderous heat without complaint, hoping still for the arrival of their noble guest. As the sun slowly set, however, concern and a growing disquiet gradually took hold. The hare was renowned not only for his abilities as a judge, but also for his reliability and punctuality. It was quite unlike him to break a promise, and the villagers understandably wondered whether some misfortune had befallen him on the road. As sunset neared they had largely abandoned hope that the case would be solved, but just as they were making ready to return home, the hare suddenly appeared. Everyone present was relieved to see that he was in excellent condition, and they were curious what could have so drastically delayed his arrival.

Although the hare's judicial competence was widely acknowledged and would never have been questioned under normal circumstances, the villagers, who knew of his notable penchant for punctuality, peppered him with questions about what had detained him. Fortunately the hare was in no way offended, but promptly provided an explanation: He had been on his way to the assembly just as planned when he suddenly spied a sand hill glowing red in the middle of a river. It had caught fire, and was fully ablaze. Noticing a rattan basket in the vicinity, he had filled it with water and tried to quench the fire, but it had taken him until evening to do so. Although several villagers found the justification a little odd, the sly neighbor understood that this unlikely story was really some kind of test, and he jumped at the chance to demonstrate his intellectual acumen. He refuted the hare's excuse with the argument that it made no sense for a sand dune that was surrounded by water to catch fire. Furthermore, he pointed out, it would be impossible to transport water in a rattan basket, since it would simply leak through the gaps between the slats. He could not possibly have put out the fire in this way. In closing, the hare's story stood in contradiction to the laws of nature and could not therefore be true.

The hare was extremely pleased to hear these words. He congratulated the farmer on his keen powers of comprehension and on his insights into the laws of nature. The farmer basked proudly in the hare's praise. Given that he had demonstrated beyond a doubt his firm grasp on the detailed workings of nature, the hare went on, he would certainly recognize that the assertion that a cow had given birth to a foal and a mare to a calf did not correspond to the laws of nature. And in order to bring the exasperating matter to a close, the hare insisted that the clever farmer return the foal to its rightful owner. The villagers were overjoyed to see the altercation put to rest so justly and in such an astonishing way—the sly neighbor had furnished the decisive argument himself. No wonder the hare is the first choice in the animal kingdom whenever a judge is needed to settle a dispute.

Mouse and Elephant

One afternoon Mouse and Elephant met in the jungle and fell to chatting about things they had seen and done. As they clambered over the roots of mighty trees and beat their way through the thick undergrowth, the elephant told the following tale:

"Earlier today I was walking along minding my own business when I suddenly heard a heavy stomping. I caught sight of a vicious elephant I know. Hoping to avoid him, I turned and ran behind a dense stand of trees. As I did so one of the lower branches gouged a serious cut in my back. You can see that it is more than two feet long."

"I'm sure that hurts," opined the mouse. "But with all due respect, my dear Elephant, please recall that you were never in mortal danger—neither the elephant nor the branch could have killed you—whereas I was hunted by a wildcat today. She nearly caught me, too! One of her claws left a large wound in my side. You will see that it is at least two feet long."

The elephant smiled. "As much as it pains me to accuse you of lying, I can't help but observe that your whole body, from the tip of your nose to the tip of your tail, is not even one foot long. How do you reconcile that with your story of a two-foot scratch?"

"Mark these words, my large friend," the mouse answered. "To each his own foot! You may measure your scrapes with your large feet, but then you must in turn allow me to measure my injuries with my own little paws."

How the Thrush Lost Her Colorful Plumage

There was a time when the thrush's feathers were not black, as they are today, but glistened in all imaginable hues. Back then, one might often see the thrush joyfully winging through the forest, leaving behind her an explosion of shimmering colors. She was especially close friends with an owl who made her home in a large hollow tree. The unlikely pair were often seen flitting through the thick underbrush searching for tasty fruits and delighting in each other's company.

Each night at sunset, exhilarated by the prospect of the cool evening air, the thrush would begin to sing out lovely melodies with her bewitching voice. This was for the owl an unmistakable sign that it was time for her to leave her resting place and join her friend in swooping through the forest. One evening, however, as the little songbird perched on the edge of her nest and trilled an especially beautiful composition, the owl did not appear. This was extremely unusual. The thrush waited awhile, but alas it was in vain. When the next evening she sang the owl's favorite song and she still did not appear, the small bird began to worry about her friend.

Fearing something dreadful had happened to her companion, she took a detour through the forest to the owl's nesting place.

As she drew near but while yet some distance away she noticed a brightly shining light directly behind the entrance to the hollow tree trunk. The glow had a magical effect that transfixed her with such a strong power of attraction that she completely forgot to make her presence known as she approached. She peeked into the tree cavity and what she saw took her breath away. There in her friend's nest she found a pile of precious gems so numerous that they spilled over the edge and littered the floor of the hollow tree. Surprised by the unexpected arrival of the thrush, the owl was struck dumb and could only sit there gaping with a distrustful air. Warily, she asked her friend why she did not let her know that she was coming. The thrush assured her that she had come with the best of intentions: She wanted to see if all was well; she had missed their nightly outings. Now she was relieved to find that no ill had befallen the owl, but rather unbelievable good fortune. Unable to comprehend the riches that lay before her, the little thrush asked her companion how she came to possess this grand treasure. Before answering, the owl peered through the tree branches to make sure that her friend had actually come alone and that nobody was within earshot. When she was sure no one else was listening she made the thrush swear to reveal the secret to no one. Only then did the owl explain how she was able to obtain the jewels.

One night while hunting, thanks to her notoriously excellent eyesight and sense of hearing, the owl heard unusual sounds and decided to investigate. She followed the sounds to the outermost edges of the forest, where she discovered a strange light that illuminated the surrounding forest floor, bathing it in a soft glow. She felt the same overpowering attraction emanating from the light that had pulled the thrush toward the owl's nest. The source of the glowing light, she discovered, was coming from inside a cave. Entering the cave, she saw, to her astonishment, that it was filled from top to bottom with gemstones. Looking around and seeing no one, she immediately set to work gathering as many as she could carry. Her greed proved greater than her own strength, however, as the stones turned out to be so heavy that even with her formidable size, she was unable to carry them all. Panting with exertion and gasping for air, she was finally able to reach the entrance of the cave with her loot, only to discover that the opening was blocked. The ogre tasked with guarding the cave and its treasure had returned. In fear of retaliation from the huge monster that had just caught her red-handed, the trembling owl immediately dropped her prize. The helpless bird shuddered as the ogre loomed over her and she felt his hot breath. With a booming voice amplified even further by the cavernous echoes, he berated her avarice and pointed out that the plunder she intended to steal was far too heavy for her to carry back home. Surprisingly, the ogre refrained from punishing her for the theft. Quite the contrary. Considering that the cave, filled as it was with jewels, did not offer him enough living space, he made her a generous offer. Under the one condition that she not become greedy, he would give her some of the gems to keep. He would allow her to come each day and help herself to the treasure, provided that the amount she took never exceeded her own body weight. Should she fail to keep this agreement, a punishment would follow, and the offer would be rescinded, the ogre warned.

Since then, the owl had returned to the cave every day to collect her gift. She was careful to take only the permissible quantity of jewels. This activity had kept her so occupied over the past few days that she had been unable to accompany her friend during their usual excursions in the forest. As the owl told her amazing story, the little thrush listened intently, ogling the owl's glittering treasure all the while. How lovely it would be to have some of those shining jewels, she thought longingly. When the owl finished her story, the thrush was unable to resist asking her friend whether she might also be allowed to share in these unforeseen riches. The owl supposed it was possible, as long as the ogre's conditions were upheld and only the specified amount of stones were removed from the cave each day. She reminded the thrush that breaking the rule would provoke the ogre's wrath, put an end to his generosity, and forever cut them off from access to the treasure. Without hesitation, the little thrush promised the owl that she would adhere to the ogre's rules and never take more than the allotted amount.

As soon as they could, the owl and thrush flew together to the cave of amazing treasure. The little thrush could only stare in wonder at the great mountain of glittering gems, which was even larger than she could ever have imagined. Very careful to follow the ogre's instructions, the friends began to search the cave for the very finest gems, whereby they made sure that neither of them took more than their own weight in stones. When they were finished, in spite of all the excitement, the thrush could not help but notice that the owl's load was much greater than her own. Undoubtedly, the reason for this lay in the fact that the owl's weight and stature greatly exceeded those of her tiny companion. Fortunately, the thrush was so thrilled with her sparkling treasure that she was able to shake off the envy that briefly arose in her and console herself with the thought that her bundle would be much lighter to carry than the owl's.

From then on each day the small thrush returned to the cave, sometimes accompanied by the owl, but also sometimes alone, and she always made sure that the weight of her stones never exceeded her own body weight. Yet she found it increasingly difficult to suppress the thought that the owl was able to take more jewels each time she visited the cave. Bit by bit this thought grew in her mind from a small trickle to a mad rushing river that consumed her every moment. When she could no longer stand the injustice, she decided to act. After all, the owl's size gave her an unfair advantage in this arrangement. It wouldn't hurt anyone if she just once took more than her own weight in stones, the thrush decided. It would be a way to set things right.

Firm in her resolution to ignore the ogre's restrictions, the thrush loaded herself down with a pile of precious stones that greatly outweighed her. When she had enough, she hurried with her heavy load to the cave entrance. Before she could reach it, however, from the dark recesses of the cave, the ogre suddenly appeared before her. He was a dreadful sight; sparks flew from his eyes and he glowed red with anger. The one condition he had put on his generosity had been broken. Petrified, the little thrush released her ill-gotten spoils and attempted to fly as fast as her wings could carry her toward the exit. But she was not quick enough to escape the wrath of the ogre. He opened his mouth and spewed out fire, turning the cave into a sea of flames that surrounded the fleeing thrush. As her splendid plumage ignited, the little thrush reeled midflight and sank to the cave floor, where she rolled in the damp earth trying to smother the flames. Only after the last of her shimmering vibrant feathers were charred an ashen gray was she able to extinguish the blaze.

Although her extraordinary voice remained, her magnificent outward appearance became once and for all a thing of the past: the price she paid for her greed. Now, if one should happen upon the inconspicuous thrush in the woods, one may be forgiven for overlooking this drab little creature whose song holds such magical powers.

The Just King

There once lived a king who was renowned throughout his realm and even beyond it for his incorruptible sense of justice. It was widely known that no one could buy his favor and that his judgments always adhered strictly to the letter of the law.

When the news arrived that one of his wives had borne him a son, he declared, deeply gratified, that this child would one day be king.

Later that very day the monarch learned that he was the father of yet a second infant boy, and he decreed that this younger child should be the crown prince. Furthermore he announced that he would step down from the throne to become a hermit at a monastery in the mountains the day his sons turned eighteen.

On their eighteenth birthday the two young men were preparing for the coronation. The sky was a deep, vibrant blue; the sun stood directly over the castle. When the future ruler noticed this, he lifted his bow and arrow, aimed for the sun, and cried, full of arrogance: "Who dares to put themselves above us and thereby to look down on us?"

"The sun is our mother," one of the king's ministers chided him. "You should kneel humbly before her and be thankful."

The young man did as he was told.

A short time later a crane was circling the palace. When the younger prince spotted it, he bent his bow, aimed, and cried, full of arrogance: "Who dares to fly above us, the future king and crown prince, and thereby to look down on us?" With one well-aimed arrow he shot the bird out of the sky.

When the crane's wife learned of her husband's death, she flew to the king. Outraged, she recounted what had happened and demanded justice.

The king summoned his ministers and his two sons to inquire whether the accusation was correct. Everyone confirmed the bird's testimony. Full of remorse, the crown prince pleaded for mercy. But the father knew no pity. With a heavy heart the king pronounced the sentence as dictated by the law: His younger son must be put to death.

The older brother objected, saying that he himself was to blame. Had he never threatened the sun with his reckless, haughty gesture, it would never have occurred to the younger brother to do something similar. By law he must also be executed for inciting a murder.

It nearly broke the king's heart. But no one was above the law, not even his sons, and so his firstborn, too, was condemned to die. Both sentences were to be carried out the following day.

Early in the morning there was already a considerable crowd gathered by the scaffold. The people were grumbling because many considered the sentences too severe.

As the executioners led the two princes into the square, a loud murmur went through the crowd. Both mothers came forward on their children's behalf, fell on their knees, and begged tearfully for leniency. The onlookers echoed their pleas, but the headsmen would not be moved. The law was the law. Judgment had been passed.

The two princes, bound hand and foot, were made to kneel. The calls for clemency grew louder. When the first executioner lifted his ax, the throng stormed the scaffold and disarmed the two men in an outright brawl.

With bloody noses and gaping wounds, it was now the executioners' turn to plead their case. Surely it would not be long before the crane's widow learned that her husband's killers had not been executed, they insisted. She would appeal to the king and they, the executioners, would pay the price. Then one of them had a brilliant idea: He asked the people to retreat for a time so that they would have an opportunity to deceive the bird. The two princes, having been smeared with the blood of the executioners, lay down on the spot where they were meant to have died.

No sooner had they taken their positions than the crane's widow flew into view. She circled over the empty square and saw the two young men lying there covered with blood. Satisfied, she turned away. Justice had been served, and now she was ready to be quit of the land where she had lost her husband.

Her powerful wings beat the air as she flew away, never to return.

The Blacksmith's Children

In the town of Tagaung there once lived a respected blacksmith. He was a hardworking man, a master of his craft with a powerful physique. It came as no surprise that a man of such gifts would have a son renowned for his bear-like strength, a giant named Maung Thin Htet, "The Strong Man."

Visitors came from near and far to marvel at Maung Thin Htet, and tales of his unusual strength spread like wildfire through the whole country until they reached the king's palace.

Tagaung Min, the king of Tagaung, was disquieted by the stories of Maung Thin Htet's unparalleled feats. He feared the blacksmith's son could pose a threat to the throne, and this thought gave him no rest until he concluded that the danger could best be mitigated by having the man arrested, and so he ordered his soldiers to capture Maung Thin Htet.

Fortunately, Maung Thin Htet was very well known in this region, and it did not take long for the king's plan to reach his ears. By the time the soldiers got to his house, he had fled deep into the jungle. The blacksmith's son had nothing to fear in the nearly impenetrable forest, where his strength and familiarity with the terrain easily protected him from the wild animals.

When the king realized that he had missed his chance to capture the strong man he devised a new plan to seize him. Instead of following him into the jungle, he would lure him out of his hiding place. To this end he paid a visit to Maung Thin Htet's father, the blacksmith, at his home. The smith, astounded by the royal visitor, gaped at his ruler much longer than appropriate. The king, meanwhile, confided that he wished to take the blacksmith's daughter, Shwe Myethna, the beautiful sister of Maung Thin Htet, as his wife.

The starry-eyed craftsman, flattered by the king's proposal, suspected nothing; he had neither reason nor recourse to deny such a powerful suitor, and so the wedding took place without delay. The king bestowed upon his bride the title Thirisanda and took her home to his elegant palace.

Knowing that the two siblings were close, he told his new wife that in honor of their marriage he wished to make peace with her dear brother and to offer him an important and coveted position in his court. Shwe Myethna had a good heart and always the best intentions, so she saw no reason to doubt the king's motives. Filled with joy, she sent word to her brother bidding him come to the palace.

Upon learning that his sister was now the king's wife and that he had been summoned to the palace to accept an official court position, Maung Thin Htet assumed that whatever he had done to incur the king's wrath had now been forgiven. He rejoiced at the prospect of seeing his beloved sister and serving her husband the king. Scarcely had the unwitting man reached the outskirts of the city, however, when he was surrounded by the king's soldiers. They bound him hand and foot, gagged him, and threw him into the palace dungeon.

Shwe Myethna never found out that her brother had been apprehended. She awaited his arrival with great anticipation. Meanwhile, the king asked her to accompany him early the next morning on his inspection rounds through the expansive palace grounds. At that time in this kingdom it was common practice to execute prisoners suspected of treason by burning them at the stake. As the king and Shwe Myethna reached a bend in the path they saw in the distance a huge fire at the foot of a champak tree that was already engulfed in flames. For a while the blaze obscured the view of the criminal, writhing in agony as the relentless flames licked at his body. The king and Shwe Myethna slowed their gait and stared at the scene, transfixed. Suddenly, as he was drawing his final breaths, the man bound to the tree caught a glimpse of his sister standing by the king's side. For all he knew, both were attending his execution. Convinced that his beloved sister had betrayed him, his heart ceased beating even before the flames could finish their deadly work.

At the very same moment Shwe Myethna recognized her beloved brother, and the extent of the king's deceit became clear to her. Before anyone could stop her she ran to her brother and threw herself into the blaze. Her body succumbed instantly to the fire but her beautiful face remained untouched. The siblings died together.

The brother and sister were then reborn as malicious nats who returned to occupy the charred remains of the tree beside which they had perished. They hid in the trunk and pounced upon any unsuspecting travelers who chanced to pass by. Their perpetual presence was a constant annoyance to the king because they reminded him of the role he had played in their violent deaths. So he ordered that the tree be felled and thrown into the river to be carried off by the capricious currents of the Irrawaddy.

When it was done, the dead tree drifted until it came to rest on a bank not far from the kingdom of Bagan where a kind king named Thinligyaung reigned. Freed as they were from the realm of the murderous king, the two *nats* forsook their quest for revenge and longed instead for a safe haven. That night the *nat* siblings appeared to the king of Bagan in a dream. In exchange for his protection they swore their services to him as guardian spirits.

The next morning the king went down to the river, where, as foretold in his dream, he found the charred remnants of the tree. The log was carried in a festive procession to the top of the extinct volcano Mount Popa, where it was then split into two equal-sized pieces. From these halves were carved sculptures of the two dead siblings, who were known from then on as Min Mahagiri, the "Rulers of the Large Mountain." Remembering the *nats'* request to serve as guardians of the kingdom, the king had two additional statues made and placed in shrines on either side of the Tharabha gate that led into the city of Bagan. Since then, everyone who passes through that gate brings an offering to the two guardians and requests their protection on their travels.

The Little Snail

Once there was a little girl who had always been a poor student. Even though she worked hard, she found her lessons difficult and often felt discouraged.

One day the teacher assigned some especially challenging homework. The girl sat down at the table as soon as she got home, for in truth she was extremely diligent. Even so, her resolve soon diminished. Her dejected eyes began to stray from her work, and she lost all focus. Staring off into space, she noticed a snail who had apparently taken a notion to climb a pole. The snail was just halfway up when she lost her grip and fell with a gentle *plop.* But look, she was already making a second attempt.

Things went on this way for a while, and the girl became completely engrossed in this admittedly lengthy drama. The snail had just fallen for the umpteenth time and was already making another attempt to climb that pole, inch by inch. The girl was expecting to hear another *plop* at any moment, but the snail climbed higher and higher. And at long last the snail had done it! The girl could hardly believe her eyes.

The student was overjoyed for the little animal, but then her eyes fell again on her woefully empty sheet of paper. Inspired by the snail's triumph—it really had overcome several setbacks to get to the top of that pole—the girl returned to her work with renewed enthusiasm. She wrote and wrote, and whenever her courage began to fail, all she had to do was think of that little snail.

The next day the girl eagerly turned in her assignment, and after the teacher had read through all the papers, she announced with surprise, though not without pride, that the otherwise poor student had written the best essay in the class.

A Troop of Monkeys and One Greedy Neighbor

An old farmer once lived a toilsome life all alone on the outskirts of a village. He tended two fields, one rice and the other corn, and he worked from sunrise till sunset just to keep from starving. His yield would have provided a decent living, except that each year at harvest time a troop of monkeys would plunder his fields. Whenever the old man approached to chase them away, they would hide or simply run to the other end of the field. They were quick and the farmer was no longer fast enough to catch them.

Finally at his wit's end, he cooked up a ploy to be rid of the monkeys.

One evening he picked some fruits that he knew were a favorite treat of the monkeys. He ground them with a mortar and pestle, rubbed the paste all over his body, and lay down in the middle of his field pretending to be dead.

The next day the monkeys returned and approached curiously. They sniffed at him and thought he smelled quite nice. A few licked his skin and thought he tasted delicious. Because the old man did not move a muscle, they believed him to be dead and decided to carry him back to their cave to eat him in peace.

They carried him across the field and into the jungle, where they swung with him through the treetops until they reached their hidden den. There they laid him on a table and contemplated how best to divide up their prize. The farmer opened his eyes just enough to see that the cave was filled with stolen treasures that the monkeys had hoarded. He sprang up and screamed as if he was out of his mind. The monkeys were so frightened that they fled. Taking his time, the farmer inspected his surroundings, took a drum and a sack of gold coins, and returned to his village.

The farmer's sudden rise to affluence aroused the suspicions of one of his neighbors. He wanted to know how it had happened and the guileless old man recounted what he had done.

The neighbor sorely wanted his own share of the monkeys' treasure, and he decided to use the same trick.

The monkeys did not take long to appear. They sniffed and licked and decided to attempt once more to carry the body to their cave. Once in the jungle, they scaled the trees and swung with him from treetop to treetop. Ants had crawled onto the farmer's body, however, and they now began to tickle and itch. At first he was able to ignore the sensation, but soon he began to twitch and scratch. The monkeys were so surprised at this that they released their grip on him. The greedy neighbor crashed through the branches to the forest floor and broke his neck.

Nan Ying and Her Little Brother

Long ago a widower lived with his two children in a house on the edge of the forest not far from the sea. The daughter's name was Nan Ying, and her little brother was called Khun Sue. Despite their mother's untimely death, the children were getting along fairly well until their father remarried and their stepmother moved in. The stepmother hated them both and wished only to live alone with her new husband and to have her own children with him. She convinced the father to send the children into the woods to search for mushrooms. Hopefully they would get lost or poisoned. But when evening came, there they were at the door of the hut.

Next the father went with them into the forest, where, with the help of a ladder, they climbed to the top of the tallest tree. The father told them stories, and the children were delighted finally to have him to themselves again. Eventually, however, they felt drowsy, and as soon as they had fallen asleep, the father climbed down and took the ladder with him.

It was pitch-black when the children awoke. They were very frightened and cried bitterly. Fortunately, the kindly forest spirits heard their sobbing, helped them down from the tree, and set them on the right path for home.

The next day, under the pretense of showing them some natural wonder or other, their father lured them again into the woods. He led them to a rocky precipice and pushed them over it from behind. What he did not know was that water had gathered at the bottom of the pit into which the children now fell. They clung tightly to each other and wept bitterly, but the forest spirits came again to their aid. They brought a large flock of birds to land on a bamboo stalk that stood beside the pit. The bamboo bent and bent until it reached down into the pit so that the children could climb up and out.

Because they had no one else in the world, and because they had no idea what else to do, they went back home and knocked timidly at the door. When their father opened it he could hardly believe his eyes. He pretended to be immensely relieved. He told them how glad he was to see them again and promised to look after them more carefully from then on.

As proof of his good intentions he offered to take them on an outing by the sea. When they arrived at the beach, however, their father abandoned them yet again, this time claiming that he was going to gather firewood. The children sat in the sand waiting and waiting.

Unfortunately for them a wicked troll lived in a nearby grotto. At the sight of the two children sitting alone by the sea the troll's mouth began to water. He disguised himself as a woman and invited them into his cave to await their father's return.

Fearing the deep black water in the fading light, the children gratefully accepted the troll's invitation. Khun Sue was still quite young, and he continued to cry even after they were in supposed safety. Nan Ying tried to be brave, and with a heavy heart she went along with the woman's suggestion to let the little boy sleep in her bed so that she might comfort him. Nan Ying herself lay down in front of the door in the next room.

Of course the troll had been planning the whole time to devour the little boy. When he removed his costume and made a move toward Khun Sue, the boy was again terrified and whimpered loudly so that Nan Ying heard it outside the door.

"Why is my brother crying?" she called.

The troll clapped a hand over Khun Sue's mouth and answered in a falsetto voice: "He got some mosquito bites, deary. Don't worry, he's fine." When Nan Ying lay back down to go to sleep, the troll gobbled up every last bite of the little boy.

The next morning the door opened and Nan Ying asked where her little brother was.

"He's safe," the troll answered cheerfully, once again disguised as a woman. "Don't worry, little one." Then he instructed the girl not to enter his room, and off he went into the forest.

Of course Nan Ying went straight into the troll's room to look for the little boy, but all she found was his bones. Filled with dread and grief, she gathered up her brother's remains and fled. She paused only long enough to pluck three leaves from the little bushes outside the troll's cave.

From a distance the troll saw the girl making her escape, and he gave chase. Nan Ying threw the first leaf. A wind storm arose and briefly kept her pursuer at bay.

Soon enough he was gaining on her again, so she threw the second leaf. Where the leaf hit the ground a waterspout formed and knocked the troll off his feet. Unfortunately he was back up in a wink and still right on her heels. Nan Ying appealed to every higher power she knew of and tossed the last leaf. A violent burst of flame shot into the air and incinerated the troll.

Being now at the end of her strength, the girl dragged herself to a pond in the woods. She washed herself in its waters, weeping disconsolately all the while. She had nothing and no one—no home, no parents, no brother. Where could she turn? What would become of her? She gazed despondently at the smooth surface of the water. Suddenly it began to ripple, and Nan Ying was frozen with terror when all at once a noble dragon rose up out of the depths.

"Do not be afraid. I am the guardian of these waters," said the creature in a low, mellifluous voice. "Tell me what troubles you, child."

Nan Ying told the wonderful dragon everything—how their father had repeatedly abandoned them, how her brother had fallen victim to the murderous troll, and how she now sat at the edge of this pool, utterly alone in all the world.

The dragon reflected awhile, and then his eyes fell on the bundle of Khun Sue's bones. He glided toward them and touched them gently with his moist snout. Suddenly the bundle began to glow. A blinding light shone so brightly that Nan Ying had to close her eyes. When she opened them again, there stood her brother, alive and well!

The overjoyed children fell into each other's arms.

"My dear ones," said the dragon in his deep, musical voice, "go to the village on the far side of this pond. Over there, you see? You will be welcomed with open arms. And if not...well, just tell them I'm the one who sent you." The dragon winked at them and disappeared headfirst into the water.

The Fear Virus

A traveler was once journeying through the hilly eastern countryside of Burma. He had just walked from one village to the next when he came upon a farmer selling his goods beside the path. Now, it is not uncommon in Burma, a country of many different peoples and tribes, for a traveler not to know the language of a local minority group. The traveler heard the merchant but could not understand him. Nor were the farmer's wares on display, because the farmer lived only a few yards away and would fetch the items from his hut upon request.

Under the circumstances, the traveler started with Burmese because it is understood by most of the population. "What are you selling?" he asked in that language.

Now the merchant understood what the traveler was asking, but he spoke Burmese with such a strong accent that his answer, "rice" (in Burmese *sunn*), sounded to the traveler's ears like *sinn*. And *sinn* means "elephant"!

The traveler looked around in fright. He took the merchant's reply as a warning about a wild elephant and ran off in a panic. Seeing the fear in the stranger's face, the startled farmer took to his heels and ran right after him.

The sun shone mercilessly down on both of them; the path was uneven and dangerous, and the hot midday sun was oppressive. Yet each time the traveler glanced over his shoulder, he saw that the man behind him was still running. The farmer, for his part, did not want to stop until the man in front of him felt that the mysterious danger had passed, and so he continued to run with all his might.

After an hour they reached a village where they collapsed from sheer exhaustion. They lay unconscious on the dusty ground as water was poured into their mouths. The villagers then lay them in the shade, and as they came to, they peppered them with questions. Had they been robbed? Chased by a wild animal?

Completely spent and out of breath, the traveler told them about the farmer's warning. The bystanders immediately turned to the other man and asked him if he had truly seen a wild elephant.

The farmer, utterly bewildered, said he hadn't and soon the misunderstanding was resolved. Only one question remained: Why then had the farmer also fled?

All eyes were on him, but he could only shrug his shoulders in embarrassment. "I was just following him."

On the Rationality of Astrology

Long ago in northern Burma there was a village with two monasteries, one in the south and the other on the northern border. Both monasteries had impeccable reputations. Each was home to numerous monks and novices; each received many visitors from the village who came to pray or offer alms. Even so, there was a spirit of rivalry between the two, as well as between their abbots, both of whom were learned, wise, and pious. At the heart of their rivalry was the following disagreement: The abbot of the southern monastery believed firmly in the power of the stars, while the northern abbot thought astrology was a fraud.

On one occasion the king invited both monks to participate in an important ceremony in Ava, the capital of the realm. After consulting the stars, the southern abbot declared that he would set out on the following day, a choice especially favored by the heavens. The other abbot snorted scornfully when he heard this news. He had heard from astrologers that the day after tomorrow would be particularly inauspicious, and for that very reason he settled on that day for his own departure.

The monks of the southern monastery selected a white boat—a color they considered to bring good fortune—and set out with their abbot for Ava. The day passed uneventfully, and toward evening they looked for a village where they could land and spend the night. The inhabitants welcomed them warmly, and soon the village elder came forward and addressed the southern abbot: "Your eminence, our village regretfully finds itself in a difficult situation. A Buddhist ceremony will take place for my son tomorrow, but the abbot of our own monastery is too ill to conduct it. May I humbly but urgently request that you delay your departure until midday tomorrow? Ava, the Golden City, is but three hours from here and you will arrive there in more than good time." Loath to deny the man, the abbot agreed. He and his retinue then spent the night in the village.

The next morning, just as the ceremony was beginning, the northern abbot and his retinue were setting out from their own monastery. Out of flagrant disregard for superstition, the northern monk had painted his boat black, supposedly an ill-fated color. The abbot scoffed at such notions, just as he did at the reputed power of the stars. And so his boat embarked on its journey down the Irrawaddy.

There was a strong wind on the river, and the northern monastery's black boat fairly raced across the water. Soon they were passing the landing where the southern monastery's white boat still bobbed at its moorings. They quickly overtook the southern delegation and sped on down the river. After one more hour of breakneck sailing it finally happened: The pitch-black boat struck a rock and shattered to pieces. The entire crew—luckily none were lost—soon stood shivering and exhausted on the banks of the river, casting accusatory glances at their abbot. He had put all of them in danger by mocking the stars, and they had very nearly paid with their lives for his impudence.

While the northern abbot stood looking upriver, his heart heavy with guilt and self-recrimination, the southern monastery's boat soon came into view. Like the black boat before it, the white boat was sailing extremely fast, too fast in fact, for it, too, soon struck a rock and capsized. Again everyone on board survived, and the southern monks were soon standing onshore beside their northern brothers. The northern abbot did not have much to say. He merely smiled knowingly, turned to his companions, and said: "And so in the end we will present ourselves to the king together—wet and muddy like canal rats."

On Sharing

A brother and his sister lived alone in a village, their parents having passed away a long time before. They had no one to look after them and were so poor that they often went hungry. With each passing year they hoped that their situation would improve, but instead it only got worse. One day a famine broke out in the entire province. The rains had not come and the harvest was so small that the two feared they would starve to death.

"We only have one kyat left," the girl said to her brother. "Go to the market and buy as much rice as you can get for it. Maybe we will get lucky, and it will last us until the next harvest. Otherwise we will starve."

The boy set off for the market. Due to the drought, however, the price of rice had quadrupled, and he could afford only four small jars, too little even for the next month.

Sad and disappointed, he made his way back to the village. Suddenly he heard a cry for help from the edge of the path. He looked all around but saw nothing except a tree around whose trunk a small climbing vine had wound itself. He was just about to keep on walking when he heard the cries again, this time louder and more insistent. He walked around the tree and found an old woman completely entangled in the plant and on the verge of strangulation.

"Help me!" she called to him weakly. "This vine is going to kill me."

The boy ripped and tore at the plant with all his might until the woman was finally able to slip free.

Exhausted, they both sat down by the side of the path to rest. "I am deeply indebted to you," said the old woman. "Before you came along, so many people passed by and I called for help but no one stopped."

"You must be hungry," the boy said. The old woman nodded.

Out of compassion he invited her home with him.

In their hut the boy found his hungry sister waiting.

She was furious when she saw their uninvited guest. "What are you thinking bringing another mouth to feed? There is not enough rice even for us."

"Aren't you greedy!" he scolded. "This old woman is hungry just like we are. We are going to share the little we have with her."

Irate, the sister built a fire and set a pot of water to boil. The old woman approached her and suggested that she add only seven grains of rice.

"That will never be enough for three," the girl objected.

The old woman just nodded and smiled kindly.

Reluctantly, the young woman did as instructed, and when the rice was cooked it filled the whole pot. For the first time in a long while the two siblings went to bed on a full stomach.

And so it continued from that day on. The seven grains produced a full pot of rice, and the two siblings and their guest survived the drought well-nourished.

When the time came to resume work in the field the old woman offered to help. Together they prepared the field, planted the rice, and harvested seven times more than any previous year.

This incident did not go unnoticed. The other villagers looked upon the two siblings with envy and suspected that they were harboring a witch.

In the middle of the night they crept into the brother and sister's hut and stole their entire rice stores. The two were distraught when they awoke. "Now we will go hungry again," they lamented through their tears.

"Don't worry," the old woman reassured them. She pulled a piece of the climbing vine out of her pocket. A few ants were crawling around on it. At her signal the ants took off. More and more ants joined their number and overnight they carried all of the stolen rice back into the hut.

This made the other villagers so angry that they armed themselves with pitchforks, shovels, and hoes in order to take the rice back by force.

The siblings hid in fear in their house but the old woman threw a piece of the vine at the horde and in no time it grew into an impenetrable hedge.

At this the farmers relented and returned to their fields.

Soon thereafter the old woman disappeared without a word. The next night she appeared to the brother and sister in a dream, and they promised to offer her seven grains of rice every day.

They kept their promise. From that day onward they always had enough to eat and never suffered from hunger again.

Life's Many Tribulations

A long, long time ago there was a kingdom in Burma near Inle Lake by the name of Paya. It was governed by a benevolent king and his queen. They were good rulers, generous and wise, and they had a son named Payar Kom Mar who was not only handsome, but also modest, clever, and well versed in the eighteen arts, from literature to painting to combat. He excelled above all with the bow and arrow.

Soon after his eighteenth year, his parents declared that it was time for him to marry a lady of the court and start a family. The prince did not at all like this idea. He felt he was too young. Nor did he wish to limit his options to the small number of women his parents deemed suitable.

The prince had twice before postponed this particular obligation, and he could not bring himself to disappoint his parents a third time, so he asked for their permission to journey to Thaton in the Mon kingdom, where he hoped to make the acquaintance of a princess who was known far and wide for her beauty. His parents consented, and the young prince set off.

When he reached his destination, instead of marching into the king's palace as the exalted prince of Paya, he disguised himself as a pauper seeking an audience with the king. After several attempts and interviews with numerous ministers, he finally succeeded. The prince bowed deeply before the Mon king and humbly requested a position working in the palace. Suspicious, the king asked several questions to test the young candidate. Because he was so well educated, the prince answered all the questions satisfactorily, whereupon the king was happy to take him into his service and assign him to some minor duties.

Thanks to his abilities and perseverance, the newcomer eventually achieved the rank of minister. The king was impressed and wanted to know more about the young man's background. Now the prince told the king the truth and revealed to him his actual objective: He had come to win the hand of the princess in marriage. The king consented and the two were wed. The young prince and the beautiful, intelligent princess were very happy together, and it was not long before a son was born to them.

As time wore on, however, the prince wearied of his domestic responsibilities. He grew apart from his wife and longed to see his parents. His dissatisfaction increased until he could bear it no longer. He went to his wife and said: "It has been so long since I have seen my parents, and I miss them sorely. I want very much to visit them, but I would ask you to remain here with our little one. It is a long and taxing journey, and I will return soon." With a smile the princess granted her husband's request, asking only that he not be away too long.

And so the prince left Thaton and set off for home. His long march led him through a desolate landscape intersected by a broad watercourse. The sole inhabitant of these lands was an old hermit who had built his shelter on the banks of the river. What is more, the region was the scene of a tremendous and long-running battle. A gigantic bird incessantly sought to capture a water dragon that lived in the river. The bird would swoop down again and again, but the dragon slipped out of his clutches every time. The old hermit followed these events in silence.

When the bird eventually noticed the old man, he flew out of sight, where he transformed into human shape. In this disguise he casually asked the old man whether he knew why the dragon was always able to slip away from the bird. And indeed, the hermit had an answer: "The dragon has a magical ruby in his mouth that protects him from the bird's attacks. The bird would have to shake the dragon by the tail in order to dislodge the ruby. But tell me, stranger, why do you ask?"

But the bird had already let loose a cry of joy and returned to his true form. He clawed at the water dragon and began to shake him severely.

The prince happened along at the very moment the gem came tumbling out of the dragon's mouth. The helpless dragon begged the stranger for help. "Why do you mistreat another creature so?" the prince asked the hungry bird.

The bird flew into a rage and growled: "I, too, must eat to live. Now be gone!"

The prince felt pity for the dragon. In a flash he bent his bow and sent an arrow through the bird's heart. With his dying breath the bird swore to take his revenge in a future life.

The water dragon could not thank the prince enough. He prostrated himself before his savior and swore to come to his aid if ever he needed it. The prince had only to touch the ground three times and then call for his help. The amazed prince thanked the dragon, then went on his way.

Meanwhile the bird was indeed reborn, this time as a giant spider living in one of three caves on the edge of a vast lake. As chance would have it, a number of local *nats* frequently swam in these same waters. They loved to frolic in the lake, but on one occasion they lost track of time until it was already getting dark, so they made camp in one of the three nearby caves. When the spider saw what was happening, she swiftly trapped the *nats* in this cave with her thick webbing.

The prince was passing this lake on his way home when he heard from afar the laments of the captured *nats*. Coming closer, he could make out the spider's threads, as thick as his arm, sealing the entrance to the cave. He promised the terrified *nats* that he would hunt the spider and then free them from their prison.

The prince soon found the beast and drew his weapons. The spider quivered with rage at the sight of the prince. She recognized him immediately and could hardly wait to get her revenge. In order to intimidate her old enemy, she lifted a massive stone and split it right down the middle.

The prince did not bat an eye. "I have a special power of my own," he said serenely. Then he shot the spider right through the heart. The nearby city Pindaya gets its name from his victory cry: "Pin ku ya," which essentially means: "I have slain the spider!"

The young prince returned to the cave and cleared the webbing with his sword. The *nats* were filled with gratitude, and they offered him the hand of the youngest *nat*, a beautiful woman named Shin Mi Ya. Even at first sight the two had eyes only for each other, and the prince married her on the spot.

The couple continued on their way and stopped to rest in the shadow of an expansive tree. By an inconceivable stroke of ill luck, a large troll happened also to be resting in the vicinity of the tree. Worse than that, this troll was none other than the latest reincarnation of the foe the prince had already encountered and defeated, first as a giant bird and then as a spider. The troll caught the young man unprepared, wrenched the deadly bow and arrow from his grasp, and flung the weapons far away. Then he seized the prince and his bride and cast a heavy iron net over them.

It was a desperate moment for the two lovers. The prince looked sorrowfully at the weeping Shin Mi Ya. What should he do?

At that moment the prince remembered the dragon's promise. He struck the ground three times with his palm and called loudly for his old friend, who appeared at once. The dragon brought the prince the bow and arrows he so urgently required. Then he freed the prisoners from the iron net. Now the prince was ready to face the troll.

It was a bitter struggle in which the prince only gradually gained the upper hand. Just as he was about to deal the troll his death blow, the monster transformed yet again. All at once the prince found himself face-to-face with the legendary magician Saw Gyi. He wore a flowing red robe and brandished a long staff. Before the prince could stop him, Saw Gyi made off with Shin Mi Ya, leaving the young man behind, severely wounded.

The young *nat* Shin Mi Ya put up a spirited but unsuccessful defense. After a while she asked Saw Gyi for some water. Her kidnapper paused to rest with her beside a rushing river. He scooped water from the stream with a silver bowl for her, but she was not satisfied. She even declined to drink from the golden bowl Saw Gyi tried next. She wanted to drink the water straight from his mouth, she said.

As the wizard bent over the river, Shin Mi Ya shoved him from behind. Saw Gyi made a hasty effort to divert the waters with magic, but Shin Mi Ya cast her cloak over him so that the magician sped downstream and was soon out of sight.

Breathless, Shin Mi Ya raced back to the scene of the battle, where, alas, she found nothing but the bloodied ground. Taking a closer look, she noticed that the bloodstains revealed a trail. She followed it, nearly out of her mind with fear for her beloved prince. At the end of the trail she found him. Dead. His cheeks were still rosy, his body still warm, but he was no longer breathing. Shin Mi Ya took her husband in her arms and wept bitterly.

Shin Mi Ya's loud sobbing woke Tha Kyar Min, one of the gods who slept on a throne in Heaven high above her. He traveled down to Earth and saw the young woman in tears. To test her love, the god transformed into a lion and tried to frighten her away from the body. But Shin Mi Ya paid him no heed as she mourned her prince with unrivaled devotion. Tha Kyar Min took on the form of a tiger and even an elephant, but nothing he tried would separate her from the one she loved.

Satisfied, Tha Kyar Min put aside his tests and sprinkled the prince with water from Heaven. The prince returned to life at once, and the lovers fell into each other's arms. Tha Kyar Min returned to his own realm; his work here was done.

The couple then traveled back to the Paya kingdom. The delighted parents welcomed their son and his bride, and all the people rejoiced to see the crown prince again. What is more, a miracle occurred: From the moment of Shin Mi Ya's arrival there was no more sickness in the kingdom. Everyone who lived there enjoyed perfect health.

For a long time this miracle was greeted with enthusiasm by the people of Paya. Not everyone was pleased, however. Physicians, doctors, and healers had lost their livelihood overnight. The situation eventually got so bad that the doctors conspired with the leading court astrologer to do away with Shin Mi Ya. The esteemed astrologer suggested to the king that since the new princess's blood was obviously magical, the monarch should sprinkle it across his kingdom. It would strengthen his dynasty in ways previously unimaginable, and all other rulers would have no choice but to pay him fealty.

The king found this prospect irresistibly appealing. At the first opportunity he sent his son off to a remote corner of the realm to suppress a marauding band of rebels. No sooner had the prince left than the king prepared to seize his daughter-in-law.

The conspirators had, however, underestimated the magical prowess of the young spirit princess. Numerous intervening walls could not prevent the treacherous plot from reaching her ears. She hastened at once to her chambers, leapt out the window, and flew away! The people of Paya were duly amazed to see their new princess sailing over their heads at top speed as she fled to the safety of her own kind.

The prince, meanwhile, was pursuing his military mission. Yet everywhere he went he found only peace. No rebels, no disturbances, no trouble. Filled now with concern, the prince hastened back to the royal palace, where he searched in vain for his beloved wife. The king was disinclined to tell him what had happened, so the prince immediately set out to find her on his own. Along the way he came upon a hermit and questioned him concerning his wife's whereabouts.

The old man smiled knowingly. He had, in fact, met Shin Mi Ya. She had drunk tea with him while she rested for a spell. Then, following a sudden inspiration, she had given the old man one of her rings and asked him to give it to the prince in case he should come looking for her. The old recluse took out the ring and pointed the prince in the right direction.

Shin Mi Ya had found her way back to the land of the *nat*s, where she was warmly welcomed. She must bathe immediately, though, so strongly did she smell of the mortals among whom she had spent so much time. A number of *nat*s were then dispatched to the nearby waterhole, arriving at the very same moment as the prince. He could sense the proximity of his wife, and he made this bold prediction: If it was his fate to find Shin Mi Ya, then the last of the servants would not be able to lift her water jug.

And indeed the vessel proved too heavy for her. The prince immediately offered assistance, and as he did Shin Mi Ya's ring fell into the water. Moments later, just when she had finished bathing, the ring slipped onto her finger. Seeing this, she sprang up and embraced her father, the king of the *nat*s. Fervently she beseeched him to bring her beloved prince to her.

Of course her father was suspicious and wanted to test the prince. How on earth had he even found the legendary land of the *nat*s? Did he possess magical abilities of his own? The father assembled seven enchanting young *nat*s and lined them up with Shin Mi Ya behind a thick curtain. Each was allowed to extend only a single finger beyond the curtain. By this finger alone the prince would have to recognize his wife.

It was not easy for the prince. In the end a kindly *nat* whose sympathies privately lay with the young couple came to his aid. In the form of a golden fly he flitted back and forth between the prince and Shin Mi Ya's finger. After a while the prince decided to trust the curious insect and took hold of the finger on which it sat. The curtain was thrown back and the lovers fell into each other's arms.

Now Shin Mi Ya's father was ready to bless their bond. After some time the two returned to the kingdom of Paya. The king had died in the meantime, and the prince and Shin Mi Ya now ruled the land happily and justly.

The Power of Karma

There was once a farmer so poor he was on the brink of despair. No matter how hard he worked, he was never able to harvest enough to keep from going hungry. Whenever the crop did happen to look a little more promising, when the corn shot up and the potatoes grew strong, a mighty storm would come, or the rivers would overflow their banks and lay waste to his field. When his wife could no longer bear their poverty and left him, he lost all will to live. Determined to die, the farmer set off to look for Death. He walked through the village asking everyone he met if they knew where he might find him.

Thinking he had lost his senses, the villagers shunned the farmer. So he left the village and roamed through the province in hopes that Death was somewhere out there. Finally he reached the coast. The beach was completely empty apart from one old man who stood with both feet in the water gazing out upon the ocean.

"Where are you headed?" the old man called out when he spied the farmer.

"I'm not sure. I'm so poor that I don't want to live anymore. I'm looking for Death."

The old man shook his head. "Young man, you don't know what you are saying."

The farmer turned away disappointed and set off again without a further question. He had not gone far when he felt a cold hand on his shoulder. "Wait," he heard a dark voice say. "Where are you going? I am the one you seek."

The farmer wheeled around in surprise and before him stood the old man.

"You?" he asked skeptically. "Well then! What are you waiting for? I'm at the end of my rope. Please help me and give me what I seek."

Death looked him up and down thoroughly, and then a wide grin spread across his face. "You can't die now because your hour has not yet come. When it is time, I will come for you whether you want it or not. Then you can try to escape me, but you will not succeed."

"Can you at least tell me when the hour of my death will be?"

"One week after you leave the beach you will become a rich man. Ten years later to the day you will die. Here is a bow and some arrows." Death conjured the weaponry out of thin air and handed it to the farmer. "Use these wisely."

With these words Death turned and walked away.

"Wait!" the man called, running after him. "I have one more question." But try as he might, he could not catch him.

And so he was left standing there on the beach dumbfounded. Feeling his stomach begin to growl, he set off to find something to eat. Presently a large bird soared overhead. The farmer had never been a good archer, yet his first arrow brought the bird right out of the sky. To his surprise he saw that the bird he had killed was not a normal bird but was made of solid gold. It was so heavy that he was able to carry it to the next town only with great effort. There he traded it for a large piece of land with the most fertile ground. While he stood on his newly purchased property a second bird flew over him. He nocked an arrow but this time missed his target.

Where the arrow buried itself in the dirt a magnificent villa suddenly sprang up with rooms full of silver and gold coins. As the incredulous farmer stepped inside, he discovered the house already full of servants ready to attend to him.

Thus the poor farmer became a very wealthy yet generous man who was loved by the whole village and who lived his life to the fullest. Time passed and the man who once so longed to die now gave no further thought to mortality. His encounter with Death was completely forgotten.

Nine years and nine months had passed when one night he awoke in a cold sweat. The old man from the beach had appeared in his dream. Death's voice was as loud and clear as if he stood directly before him. The man shivered. Only three months remained before the ten years were up. But he was healthy. He loved his life. He didn't want to die. Was it possible to escape Death?

The following day he ordered his servants to build him a watertight crate and to fill it with a three-month-and-three-day supply of food and drink. They were to then bring the crate down to the beach.

When he saw the crate, doubt briefly crept into his mind. Did he really want to spend three months in such cramped quarters? It looked anything but comfortable. If this is the price I must pay to escape Death, then I am willing to pay it, the young man thought to himself with a sigh as he climbed into the crate. He instructed his servants to seal the crate, secure a long rope to it, and let it sink to the bottom of a deep part of the ocean. They were to tie the other end of the rope to a palm tree and then pull him back up onto land in exactly three months and three days.

A few weeks later, as Death was checking his list of those whose time had nearly expired, he noticed the name of the young man and immediately remembered their chance encounter on the beach. Curious as to what had happened to the young man, he set off to find him in the living world. Even though he searched high and low, the man was nowhere to be found. He double-checked his list in case he had made some kind of mistake, but no, the man's name was definitely there. He continued his search, traveling from village to village, checking in every house and every hut, but to no avail.

When the day arrived on which the young man was supposed to die, Death went back to the beach to the very spot where the two had met ten years earlier. He found no trace of him here, either. Completely at a loss and worn-out, Death walked along the beach until he suddenly tripped over a tightly drawn rope and tumbled head over heels into the sand.

What kind of an idiot would leave a rope tied up here? he wondered. He was just about to keep on walking when he was overcome by curiosity and began to pull on the rope. It was rough going. The rope turned out to be longer than anticipated, and whatever was attached to it was heavier than he had expected. Finally a wooden crate surged up from the depths and soon the waves washed it up onto the beach. He inspected the construction in amazement. He knocked on it. Hearing nothing, he opened it, and out stepped the young man.

"Ah, so here you are then!" Death said angrily. "I've run myself ragged looking for you. Did you really think you could escape your fate by hiding in a crate?"

The young man fell to his knees before Death. "Please spare me," he begged. "I will give you half of my riches if you show me mercy. I don't want to die!"

Death looked at him sternly. "Didn't I once explain to you right here on this beach that no one can die before his time has come? Didn't you listen?"

"Y-yes, I did," stammered the young man.

"No one can delay his death when the time has come, even if he very much desires to and even if he tries everything in his power. Do you know why not?"

"No."

"It is because every person has their own karma. It's the result of everything they have done in their previous existence."

The young man again began to moan, complain, and beg. Death silenced him with a wave of his hand and then began his work.

The Boy with the Harp

In the Irrawaddy delta, amid the brackish waters and the marshes, there lived a boy named Maung Shin. His father was one of the farmers in the delta who understood a thing or two about cultivating crops and breeding cattle, and the family was moderately well-off. Maung Shin was just a boy when his father died quite unexpectedly, and that was the beginning of his family's misfortunes. Maung Shin's mother did her best to keep them afloat and to stretch their savings as far as possible, but despite their modest lifestyle, their reserves were soon spent.

Maung Shin's mother had a sister who lived nearby and who had borrowed money from them before his father's tragic death. Hoping to improve their dire situation, Maung Shin's mother went to her sister and asked her to repay what she had borrowed. To her dismay, she got nothing from her sister but derision and insults. Her sister scoffed at her request and claimed to have no money. The poor widow was utterly taken aback, especially since she knew well that her sister led a carefree life, had significant means at her disposal, and would have had no trouble paying off the loan. In the end she resolved to sever ties with the family, to leave her village near Bago, and to try her luck at a fresh start with her son in some other place.

Now, even as a very young child Maung Shin had demonstrated a matchless talent on the arched harp. The tones he coaxed out of the strings were so pure and compelling that they could melt a heart of stone. On top of that he was a gifted singer whose clear voice and noble bearing reflected his honorable spirit. His melodies, drifting on a soft breeze, were inconceivably beautiful. With the family savings spent and with no other reliable sources of income on the horizon, Maung Shin took to playing harp and singing for the inhabitants and pilgrims who happened through his new village. Mother and son lived primarily from the symbolic offerings they received in recognition of the boy's widely acclaimed abilities.

Maung Shin was profoundly unhappy about this turn of events and about the financial crisis in which the family now found itself. He could hardly bear to watch his mother's daily struggle to survive, and he felt a burning desire to do more to lighten her burden and to improve the family's situation. The meager earnings from his music barely sufficed to meet even their most basic needs. Maung Shin came to the conclusion that he must find additional work if he wanted to have any hope of improving his family's fortunes. Because the lad had few talents beyond playing and singing, however, he needed to find some kind of unskilled work. Eventually he fell in with a band of lumbermen who harvested the yellow sandalwood trees in the region and who were willing to take him into their service. Sandalwood was in high demand both as a building material and for its distinctive essential oil. The loggers were on their way to the thickly wooded and often crocodile-infested islands of the lower Irrawaddy delta.

Given Maung Shin's limited skills as a woodcutter, however, the lumbermen decided that ship's cook was a better fit for the boy, who eagerly accepted the position. When he was not in the galley preparing a meal for the crew, he was out in the wilds gathering all sorts of provisions so that he would be able to serve the men a fresh, delicious meal at the end of their long, strenuous workday. While searching for ingredients, he would sometimes pause to sing and play his harp. The residents of the idyllic delta islands found his lovely notes irresistible, but these islands were also home to several treasure goddesses who were soon captivated by Maung Shin's enchanting tones. It was not long before they made a regular habit of searching out the young man. They would join him on the boat nearly every day so that they could sing and dance while he played.

When the holds were finally full of lumber, the pilot made the boat ready for the homeward journey. But when the boat was pulling away from its berth, the anchor suddenly stuck fast, and no amount of exertion could free it. The pilot and his crew investigated but could find no reason why it would not move. When all possible remedies failed, the crew supposed that one of their number must have committed some reprehensible crime during their stay on the island. Someone must have incurred the wrath of the spirits. When no one confessed, the group decided to draw lots. Every member of the crew must take one of several little rolls of paper, on only one of which was a red dot. The man with the red dot would be considered the guilty party.

When all the lots were drawn and unrolled, who should have the red dot but Maung Shin! The foreman knew that Maung Shin had done no wrong and had spent his days on the island gathering food for the crew and playing music, activities that could hardly have enraged the gods. He concluded that it must be a mistake, and the lots were gathered and shuffled for another round. When Maung Shin drew the red dot a second time, the captain and the crew again gave him the benefit of the doubt, but when Maung Shin drew the red dot a third time, there was no more getting around the fact that he was the cause of their difficulties. To appease the gods the pilot had Maung Shin thrown summarily from the boat into the muddy waters where the crocodiles lay in wait. Maung Shin died a miserable death.

If anyone was suffering pangs of guilt, they did not last long. Sacrificing Maung Shin had apparently satisfied the gods, for the boat was now able to pull away and sail for home without further incident.

The crew did not know that the treasure goddesses had prevented the ship from leaving in order to keep the lovely music on the island. It was they who had seen to it that Maung Shin drew the red dot every time. The treasure goddesses were overjoyed that they had managed to thwart his departure. They gathered his mortal remains from the river floor, and Maung Shin was transformed into a *nat*, a spirit named U Shin Gyi. To this day people will make a small offering to the young harpist before venturing out on the water, whether river, lake, or open sea. The guiltless lad came to a violent death through no fault of his own, and only through the unjust deeds of the goddesses. It is said that if one listens closely, one can still make out the unearthly tones emanating from the musician's silken harp strings amid the tumbling surf.

The Honest Merchant

In a certain Burmese village, as in many other parts of the country, there was a market every five days where farmers would come from the surrounding area to peddle their goods. It was always loud and crowded, and the air was filled with the fragrance of spices, meats, and assorted delicacies. Among these farmers was a man of the Palaung tribe. On this day, as usual, he had set up a booth where he was selling, among other things, fresh eggs. The eggs, like the chickens who laid them, came in a range of sizes.

He was doing a lively business, and of course the largest eggs were the first to go. In the end the farmer was left with only the smallest, so one of the later customers started to dicker with him. The farmer admitted that these eggs were smaller than usual and offered the customer a good bargain, but the customer continued to haggle until the farmer eventually offered such a low price that he would hardly profit from the sale.

The customer, who saw things differently, became cross. The farmer said: "I know that these are very small eggs, but I promise you that they are absolutely exquisite. Remember: I am not the one who laid these eggs. Nor did I ask the chickens to make them so small. If I could lay an egg for you it would be the size of a papaya!"

The customer recognized the farmer's sincerity and was satisfied. He purchased all of the remaining eggs and the two parted with the deepest mutual respect.

The Magic Comb

A long time ago the Karen people lived in a single village under the leadership of benevolent elders. The entire community worked, ate, and lived together like one large family. They shared everything they owned.

One harvest season, however, they found themselves in dire straits: A large wild boar kept destroying their fields, and the villagers were unable to kill it. Completely at a loss, they brought the problem before the village elder, who took it upon himself to solve it.

I am no longer the youngest, he thought, but I am and remain the leader of this community. He set off into the forest searching for signs of the wild boar. Soon he found its tracks and discovered torn-up areas on the forest floor where the animal must have foraged. At last he found the boar's den and lay down to wait near its entrance. When he could hear the quiet, even breath of the sleeping animal, he crept nearer and stabbed it to death in its den.

Upon his return, the village elder was greeted joyously. Why, they asked, had he taken on this task single-handed and thereby put himself in so much danger?

The elder only laughed: "I am old, my children. If I die it is but a small loss, don't you think?"

Out of the tusks of the wild boar, the village's best craftsman fashioned a magnificent comb, which they used on the elder's hair in a festive ceremony. But what a surprise awaited the entire village when, before everyone's eyes, the gray hair that was drawn through the comb turned black and the elder grew younger until he was once again a young man. It appeared that the Karen had discovered the secret of eternal youth.

From then on, no one in the village grew old and no one died of old age. The settlement thrived and the population multiplied and soon there was not enough space for everyone. With as much as they could carry, the Karen set out to look for new land. In the selection of their new location they relied on an adage they believed in: If you dug a hole and then filled it back up, you could supposedly judge the quality of the soil. If the surface of the ground where the hole was dug was flat, meaning that all of the dirt fit exactly back in the hole, then the soil at that spot was just right.

After a while the group reached a river. They stopped along the bank to rest and tested the ground but determined that it was not good enough. While playing in the river the children discovered an unfamiliar type of mussel. Immediately they built a fire and set a pot of water to boil. Yet no matter how long they boiled them, the mussels would not cook. After three days the elder decided that they had wasted enough time; another faction of the tribe, however, wanted to wait. In the end they agreed that those who followed the elder would leave a trail through the banana trees to mark the way they had gone.

The remaining villagers waited and waited but the mussels remained inedible. After a week they added flower petals that the children had found to the water. But the petals dissolved and turned the entire mixture into a red brew that they were afraid to eat lest they poison themselves, so they poured out the whole pot.

When finally they set out to follow the first group, they discovered that the branches that had been cut from the banana trees to mark the trail had already long since grown back! It was the rainy season when plants in the jungle grow quickly, and now the Karen could no longer see the path their brothers and sisters had taken.

So it came to pass that today there are two different tribes of Karen people. Many even believe that the elder is still out there somewhere with his magic comb and that he alone can reunite the divided tribe.

A Mother's Warning

A mother lived with her son in a farming village in Karen State. They tended a small plot, and they worked hard with nary a rest, but it sufficed only for the barest necessities. In a village of poor farmers they were among the poorest, and their neighbors looked down their noses at them.

As the son got older he fell in love with a young woman from another village whom the mother did not like in the least.

"She has the powers of a wicked sorceress," she warned.

But the son would not be dissuaded; he wanted to marry the girl.

"Don't do it. She'll bring you nothing but bad luck," prophesied the mother. "Let me give you some advice: Watch everything she does very closely, and you'll soon see that I'm right."

Despite these words, the two were wed. And yet the man was troubled by his mother's remarks. He wanted to make sure that his wife did not possess dark magic, and he came up with a way to test her.

"I've got such a hankering for mole," he said. "Do you think you could catch me one?"

"Of course," she replied, and off she went. She searched for hours, but found no mole. Instead she found a young child playing beside the path. She turned it into a mole and took it home with her, where she butchered it. With the meat she prepared a curry for her husband.

The husband, for his part, had secretly followed his wife and seen everything.

The only thing he wanted now was to get rid of his wife as quickly as possible.

"Do you love me?" he wanted to know.

"Of course I do," she replied.

He led her across the fields into the woods and finally to a cliff. "My mother has disowned us. The village has banished us. I am weary of life," he claimed. "Are you ready to die with me?"

"Yes."

"Are you willing to jump first?"

"Yes," she said, and without hesitation she leapt over the edge but got tangled in a tree only a few yards down.

Thinking her dead, the relieved husband made his way back to the village.

The sorceress spat a curse when she realized he had betrayed her. He would pay with his life for this deceit.

And so it came to pass: Before he even left the wood he was so severely mauled by a wild boar that he bled to death within minutes.

But neither could the sorceress free herself. She died a miserable death entangled in the branches of the tree, after which she turned into a stone.

The Timid Son

A long time ago in the mountains of Myanmar, a tribe of close-knit villagers lived with their chief, who was strong, wise, and respected by all. The community had a problem, however: Their future leader, the son of the current chief, was afraid of absolutely everything. As a child he had been too frightened to play alone or eat by himself; he would not even sleep in his own bed. At first the chief assumed it was only a phase, that the boy would eventually outgrow these childish quirks.

Alas, he was mistaken. While the boy did develop into a hardworking, sensible young man who soaked up all knowledge offered him, be it martial arts or literature, he never learned to put aside his fears. The father had no idea what to do about this, and he wondered how the clan would ever survive under his son's leadership.

One day the chief disappeared without a trace. He had gone into the forest and not returned. The village was in an uproar and the warriors immediately prepared to send out a search party. Hopefully nothing had happened to him.

No one even bothered to ask the chief's son; years of experience had taught them that the boy was completely useless when it came to such matters. The villagers simply walked past the chief's house casting sad and occasionally contemptuous glances through the window at the young man, who cowered motionless in his room.

As the chief's son sat alone, shame began to wash over him. It seeped into his limbs; his hands went numb, and his breathing grew shallow. Finally it took possession of his heart. Oh how his cursed cowardice mortified him! And heaped on top of it all, there came the worry about his father! It was too much to bear.

The moment finally came when his shame and concern outweighed his anxiety. Nothing could be worse, the young man decided, than sitting around like a picture of misery, and he got up. Taking up his father's bow and arrows, he strode out to meet the others.

After they got over the shock of seeing him out and about, they explained that he had to do three things to prove himself as a warrior and join their ranks. He must bring them a falcon's feather, the tusk of a wild boar, and the pelt of a panther.

The young man set off on his quest. Anything was better than remaining a prisoner to his fears. In fact, he was a good marksman, so it was not long before he brought down a falcon and put one of its feathers in his belt. After hours of hunting, just at dusk, he was also able to fell a wild boar. For his third task, he climbed a tree and lay there in wait, keeping watch all night long. This jungle was home to panthers; he had even seen one as a child, when he had wailed loudly at the sight. Most of the time, these large cats stayed far away from humans, but in the wee hours of the morning he got lucky: One of these dark, noble creatures padded silently into view and he killed it with one well-aimed shot.

Filled both with pride and with concern for his father, the young man ran back to the village. There he was honored for his accomplishments and was accepted into the ranks of the proven warriors of the clan. Naturally he asked permission to join the search for his father. The villagers gave him the task of searching a mountain known to all to be inhabited by ghosts. The only other person who ever visited this place was a shaman who spoke to these beings.

Along the way he was attacked by a masked man. The stranger jumped down on him from the trees above and pummeled him with both fists. The fight was short but fierce, and then the attacker fled. Enraged, the chief's son followed him to a dark cave. Only after he was already inside did he realize he had walked into a trap. He could barely see anything and all around him he heard the whisper of eerie voices...

Blinding sunlight suddenly streamed into the cave. When the young man looked up he saw that he stood before a long table with several chairs occupied by the elders of his village. In the middle of them all sat his smiling father!

The chief approached his son and proudly pressed him to his chest. He then turned to the group and asked, "How is it, my dear friends, that you now see before you my son, full of courage and strength?"

"It is because of the love he has for his father," answered the oldest.

"That is correct," said the chief with a nod. Beaming, he looked at his son before he continued. "I treat this tribe like a large family," he said. "Our greatest strength lies in sticking together and watching out for one another. This is the only way we can survive!"

The young man took these words to heart and tried his best to follow them. When the father died many years later, the son took over the position of chief with pride and confidence.

The Grateful Serpent

Long ago there lived a girl named Saw Nan Wai, which meant something like "Budding Blossom"—an auspicious name, but one that did not live up to its promise. The girl was from Hsipaw, a Shan city in the north of Burma. She had grown up without parents or any kind of family in a monastery where instead of care and support she got nothing but neglect and abuse. The nuns would give her the least pleasant chores, and they would scold and beat her. At some point the girl could stand it no more. She decided to flee the prison-like monastery and to seek shelter in the wilderness.

She struggled just to survive until one day she came across a hermit who dwelt deep in the forest. A big heart was the man's only possession, and he took pity on the girl wandering about lonely and frightened in the wood. He took the child into his care and looked after her. For thirteen years she served as his assistant while practicing the art of meditation. Peace now entered the life of this girl who had previously known only loneliness, sorrow, and pain. The entire time she lived with the hermit she worked hard and strove to lead a righteous and dutiful life.

The hermit, knowing well the attraction the dark woods held for sinister spirits, had impressed upon Saw Nan Wai that while gathering food she must never stray beyond the limits of a well-defined area, and she had always followed his instructions faithfully. One day, however, as she was gathering fruits and other provisions, she inadvertently overstepped her bounds. Hardly had she set foot outside the sheltered area when she ran afoul of a band of thieves who molested her and abused her so severely that she died. The final seconds of her life were dominated by a burning desire for grim revenge against her killers. Because she had yielded to her lower instincts and wished for vengeance in the final moments of her life, she was reborn not as a person but as a python.

The desperate serpent sought solace and guidance from the hermit in the forest whose beneficent instruction and tutelage had so helped her as a human child. In the meantime, however, the girl's former teacher had also died. His years of contemplative living in nature had earned him a new existence as a monk in Bago. When the python heard this she set out on the long journey in hopes of being reunited with the former hermit. Because snakes cannot travel more than a few miles each day, it was a wearisome and difficult undertaking. Eventually she reached Yangon, completely exhausted, and asked a passerby to take her to the Kyi Taung Tawya monastery in Bago. Because no one had ever heard of that monastery, a small delegation was sent to Bago in order to find out whether such a place even existed.

Once in Bago, the emissaries from Yangon visited numerous monasteries. Only after a long and arduous search did they find the monastery the snake had mentioned. It was a modest temple in a remote corner of the city with no appreciable financial resources. As soon as they arrived in the early evening they sought out the abbot and told him of the serpent's inquiry. The abbot was astonished and insisted on traveling with them back to Yangon that very evening. Despite the late hour, the python had waited anxiously for their return and wanted immediately to show her gratitude to the person who had sheltered and cared for her when she was a human child.

Try as he might, the monk at first had little recollection of his previous life. Nor was he inclined to believe that the serpent could be the young woman who had grown up under his care. During the night, however, he had vivid dreams full of images from his life as a hermit. He also remembered his young assistant, the little girl who had wandered alone through the forest. Bright and early the next morning he sought out the serpent again. With the help of a young clairvoyant he was able to speak directly with the snake. The python asked for permission to rest on his shoulders. The monk replied that if she were truly his companion in a previous life, she must now prove it by sloughing off the fetters of her weight, by diminishing her body until it weighed no more than a feather. The serpent happily fulfilled his request. She slithered with her bulky body up the monk's arm and rested a few minutes on his bony shoulders—a burden he could never have borne if the snake had retained her natural weight.

The monk from the Kyi Taung Tawya monastery was completely persuaded that the python truly was the young girl he had known in his life as a hermit. Still, he hesitated to take responsibility for the giant snake. He was no longer young, and a reptile of her size required a substantial amount of care that the impoverished monastery could ill afford, not to mention the fact that the monastery grounds were already home to a host of other animals, including several that were staples of a python's diet. When he told the serpent about his reservations, she pleaded with him not to abandon her. She swore a solemn oath to live in harmony with the other beasts. Beyond that she prophesied that the monastery would have no trouble feeding her, for food would flow into the monastery in the form of generous offerings. And so the monk agreed to take the snake into the monastery's protection as long as she would keep her word. Having reached this agreement, the monk and the snake set out that very morning for Bago. By noon they were standing at the entrance to the monastery. The snake was released and she slithered at her leisure into the ordination hall, where she resided peacefully, just as she had promised.

The news made the rounds, and since that day the monastery has experienced no shortage of pilgrims who now stream in from all parts of the country to see for themselves the grateful serpent, a sacred animal if not indeed a saint in snake's form. The visitors pay homage to the honorable creature in the hopes that she might pass on some of her power to them. Some lay money and a bit of snakeskin beside her because they believe that by direct contact some of the animal's strength is conferred on both. A portion of the money is always left behind as an offering for the snake. The pilgrims carry the rest of the money in their purses, along with the pieces of snakeskin, in order to establish an enduring connection to the serpent's magical powers.

As the python had foretold, pilgrims from near and far donated large sums of money—enough to finance the reconstruction and renovation of many stupas and temples in Bago and the vicinity.

The Starving Orphans

A long time ago, in a Danu village, there lived two orphans: a boy named Saw Shwe and his sister, Saw Ngwe. Their parents had died early on, and they were very close, but they led a harsh life. They were poor, and though they worked long hours in the fields, they were almost always hungry.

One year a terrible drought spread across the land. Three years passed without a drop of rain. The fields were parched, the rivers ran dry, and the livestock died. The villagers took to scouring the jungle for food out of pure desperation.

Saw Shwe and Saw Ngwe rationed their meager stores carefully, but in the end they were left with only one single grain of rice. Unsure how to split it, they took turns sucking on it until the sister accidentally swallowed the tiny grain. Her brother was furious and yelled at her, blaming her for their predicament. He sent her out into the jungle to look for food while he waited, half-starved, outside the door of their hut. Saw Ngwe wandered brokenhearted through the forest. She had never intended to take the last meager bit of food from her dear brother. She searched for several days, but like all of the other villagers, her efforts were in vain. Every piece of bark, every stalk, every edible berry had long ago been harvested. After sunset on the third futile day, she died of hunger, weakness, and despair.

Meanwhile, her brother still hoped for her return. He blamed himself for sending her off alone into the forest and deeply regretted his anger, but he was too weak to follow her. During the long wait, he fell asleep and never woke up. He died with a deep pain in his heart because his sister was not beside him.

After their deaths the children were reborn as tiny birds, and to this day you can find them flying about. The brother calls to his sister: "Saw Ngwe, Saw Ngwe!" And she answers with a sustained "Kyaut py, kyaut py!"—I am afraid! I am afraid!

The Flood

Some time ago an old woman lived with her two grandchildren on the outskirts of a village. The girl was nine years old, the boy seven, and their parents had died a few years earlier. Grandmother and grandchildren lived together in abject poverty, scorned by the other villagers, who looked down on them and treated them like lepers.

One day the whole village went to fish at the nearby river. As usual, the three had not been invited, but the grandmother sent the children to follow the main group. Maybe they would find someone to play with, or maybe they would form some other kind of connection to the broader community.

At the river the lines were cast, but no one was having any luck that day. The men sat for hours on the banks, their irritation growing all the while.

At some point someone recalled the old superstition that a bit of human flesh thrown into the water would draw the fish. Everyone laughed about it at first, but it stuck in their minds. One after another the inhabitants cast sidelong glances at the two children hovering shyly on the fringes. Surely they would not be missed. No one cared for that family. Weren't they orphans, anyway? Outcasts?

A couple of the men stepped menacingly toward the girl, who started to cry. The men wavered briefly, then turned to the brother, who laughed nervously, not really understanding what was afoot. Without hesitating the men snatched him up. Wailing loudly in fright, the girl ran and hid in the brush.

Back in the village the grandmother waited at the door for the return of her dear little ones. At last she saw a long line of people approaching. The villagers were coming back! The men were overloaded with fish. It looked as if they had had a bumper catch. The old woman kept a sharp eye out for her grandchildren, but they were not in the throng.

Down at the river the sister ventured warily out of hiding only after weeping for hours. She went to the water's edge, where she noticed a little shrimp floating. Had her grandmother not said that a dead person's spirit might find its new home in a nearby animal? She scooped the little creature gingerly into a bucket and ran home in tears.

Meanwhile, the grandmother was still waiting at the door of the hut for her grandchildren. She was dreadfully worried about them, for the sun was already low in the sky. Finally she saw a little girl in the distance running toward her. The girl fell into her grandmother's arms and wept disconsolately. Between sobs she managed to tell her grandmother what had happened.

A shiver ran down the old woman's spine when she heard the appalling tale. By the time the girl was finished the old woman had lost all feeling. Her hands began to tremble with rage, and she stood up. From the innermost corner of the little hut she fetched a staff that had been in the family for generations. One day it would have belonged to her grandson. The two set out together, climbing higher and higher into the mountains. It was strenuous work, but wrath drove the old woman on and on.

Eventually they found themselves atop the highest peak in the region. The grandmother took the girl in her arms and kissed her. Then she straightened up and uttered a curse in a furious voice. She cursed the people who had taken her grandson from her. She cursed the people who had been utterly without compassion or humanity. She cursed the sick, incurable world in which such a thing could ever have happened. Then, with all her might, she thrust the staff into the ground.

From their vantage point up on the mountain the woman and the girl could see clearly how the rivers over-ran their banks. How the water rose and washed over that village and all the other villages. How it engulfed field and forest and eventually reached even the mountaintop and swept it away. In the end there was nothing left but the smooth surface of the water, while the dregs of the old world now rested on the new ocean floor.

The Wise Teacher and His Student Maung Pauk Kyaing

In a small village near the city of Tagaung there lived an elderly couple with one child, a son named Maung Pauk Kyaing. The couple naturally wanted to ensure that their child received the best possible education, so as soon as they deemed him old enough, they sent him to study under a renowned teacher in Taxila. They were convinced he would obtain an education superior to any other. Unfortunately, this was not to be. As it turned out, Pauk Kyaing had no aptitude for learning. He was never able to remember his lessons, and after many years of fruitless labor the unhappy student prepared to return to his hometown and parents.

Pauk Kyaing may have been a poor student, but he possessed other remarkable traits, above all a robust physical stature coupled with a keen sense of perception. His teacher recognized this and did not want to send him home without impressing on him at least a few insights. He also wanted show that the boy's time under his tutelage had not been a complete waste.

Just before the boy began his long journey home, the teacher came to him and told him he wanted to give him one last lecture for the road. This lesson would serve him for the rest of his life. The student, who had now matured into a young man, was thankful for the guidance and listened attentively as the teacher shared three pieces of advice: "Only one who travels will reach his destination. Only one who asks will receive an answer. Only one who sleeps less will get more out of life."

Armed with this new wisdom, which he burned into his memory, Pauk Kyaing confidently set off for home. As his teacher had predicted, this journey was without a doubt the only way to get from one place to the next. Perhaps the fruitless years of apprenticeship would ultimately prove to be worthwhile on account of his teacher's advice.

After many weeks of travel Pauk Kyaing reached the region of Tagaung. The capital itself is in the Mandalay district, on the east bank of the Irrawaddy River. As he neared the metropolis he came upon a number of ministers from the king's palace, who told him that the kingdom of Tagaung was currently without a ruler. Because his teacher's parting words were still fresh in his memory and because he wanted to know more, Pauk Kyaing did not hesitate to ask about how this state of affairs came to pass.

The ministers told him that the king had been murdered some time ago and that anyone since then who had ascended to the empty throne to rule beside the widowed queen had been found dead the next morning. Understandably, the violent demise of so many had made the job considerably less appealing than it would otherwise have been. The ministers had run out of candidates and did not know where else to turn. Wondering what could have caused the death of so many hopeful young men, Pauk Kyaing volunteered to be the next candidate.

The ministers were overjoyed and also relieved. Although they were convinced that Pauk Kyaing would meet the same fate as his predecessors, the arrival of a new candidate promised to reduce the pressure on them, at least during the preparations for the new king's inauguration. With a fanfare that could be heard far and wide,

Pauk Kyaing was led to the castle, where he was met with a grand reception, as befitted his status as the future king. Numerous vats were filled with fragrant waters and then blessed. The water served to purify the body, mind, and soul in order to prepare the young man for the position of responsibility.

After the ritual cleansing, the attendants clothed Pauk Kyaing in costly robes worthy of a ruler, and they placed the king's throne next to the oft-widowed queen's. During the coronation festivities the ministers as well as the other palace spectators were highly impressed by the inner strength that emanated from this chance aspirant, even though they had clearly warned him just that morning about his possible fate. When the courtiers and ministers lined up to swear their oaths of fealty, there were many among them who were sorry that such a courageous and brave young man would no longer be among the living the next morning.

These speculators, however, did not know Maung Pauk Kyaing or the valuable wisdom he had acquired from his widely acclaimed teacher. That evening, as the monarchs prepared to retire, the newly minted king recalled his teacher's third lesson. On that advice, he fought with all his might to ward off sleep, even though it had been a long, arduous day and he was completely exhausted.

He lay awake pondering all of the possible causes for the kings' deaths. Earlier in the day he had asked questions, and as his teacher had said, he had received answers. He had learned that the bodies of the kings had been colored black, from which it was surmised that they had been poisoned. As Pauk Kyaing considered the situation, however, another scenario presented itself. What if it was not poison at all but the fiery breath and the powerful talons of a one- or many-headed *naga* dragon that had killed his predecessors?

The king devised a plan. He called in his servants and ordered them to fetch him a large amount of banana leaf stalks and a finely honed sword. As soon as the stalks had been collected the king tied them into a human-sized bundle and covered it with his clothes and a blanket so as to create the appearance that he lay sleeping in his bed. Despite his overwhelming drowsiness, Pauk Kyaing followed his mentor's advice and resisted the urge to sleep. Instead, he withdrew to a corner of the bedroom and hid behind heavy curtains while waiting to see what would happen. The night passed ever so slowly. The waiting seemed endless, and the quietness of the castle only heightened the oppressive eeriness of his situation. Just when he could no longer fight off sleep and was on the verge of abandoning his hiding place, he heard a soft scraping. It sounded as if something heavy were being dragged back and forth along the tiled palace floor. The noise grew louder—someone or something was clearly coming nearer.

Pauk Kyaing peered out from behind the curtain just in time to see a *naga* of frightening proportions gliding into the room. He cast a broad shadow by the light of his own fiery-red eyes, and in their glow Pauk Kyaing could make out the endless sparkling rows of scales along the mighty tail he whipped from side to side at every step. The moment he entered the bedchamber, the dragon sprang onto the man-sized bundle, assuming it was the king. His deadly claws sank into the supple foliage of the banana trees, where they caught fast. Desperately the *naga* struggled to free himself. Pauk Kyaing, who had been watching the events, rushed toward the dragon sword in hand and struck him with powerful blows. The would-be assassin writhed in pain and rage, but Pauk Kyaing finished him off, hacking his body to pieces. Only when the dragon lay still before him did he allow himself to fall asleep.

The next morning the king's servants entered the bedchamber with great trepidation. They expected to find the mortal remains of yet another tragic victim. How surprised and overjoyed they were to learn that Pauk Kyaing had not only survived the night, but also managed to defeat the monster responsible for so many violent deaths.

For his ingenuity, daring, and heroic bravery, Pauk Kyaing was rightly celebrated as a true and distinguished ruler.

The pieces of the *naga*'s corpse were collected and brought before the queen. When she saw these proofs of the monster's death she was beside herself. In the meantime it had become obvious that the *naga* had been the queen's secret lover. Together the two had conspired to dispense with anyone who came between them. Knowing well that such treachery was punishable by death, the queen made a crafty proposal in order to escape conviction. Hoping to regain the king's trust, she feigned gratitude to him for defeating the *naga*, who, as she now claimed, had forced himself upon her every night. She asked the king to postpone her execution and to solve a riddle of her own contrivance within a limited amount of time. Should he succeed, she would face her death; otherwise he must pardon her and die in her place.

Being a just king, and feeling disinclined to execute a woman of royal blood, Pauk Kyaing generously agreed. Perhaps he let himself be put to the test because he felt sure he would prevail. He had, after all, solved the mystery of the king's murder, which no one else had been able to do. But when the queen, known for her craftiness, recited the riddle, Pauk Kyaing regretted his generosity. It went like this: "One thousand for the skinning, one hundred for the sewing, skin for a pillow, and bones for hairpins."

Pauk Kyaing thought hard, but he was unable to decipher the meaning of the words, however much he tried.

As the days passed and there was still no answer in sight, the king's subjects grew anxious. They did not wish to lose another ruler, especially one who had proven himself to be so noble and fearless. When only one day remained to solve the queen's riddle the whole land was close to despair; the impending deadline and the consequences of missing it were discussed at every gathering in the kingdom, even among the animals.

Meanwhile Pauk Kyaing's parents had been missing their only son, but the news of the new king spread quickly, and when they heard of his heroics and his coronation, they hurried see to him.

Along the way, tired from the arduous journey, the old couple decided to rest and to eat their midday meal under a shady tree. The crumbs from their provisions attracted some crows. These birds, having always been inclined to chattiness, seemed particularly talkative that day. Since the couple came from a small village, where man and nature are closely connected, they were familiar with the behavior of the animals and could even communicate with some of them. When the crows came within earshot, the parents were amazed to hear that they were talking about their son, the newly crowned king. In this way they learned of the disaster that threatened to ruin him.

Deeply worried, they hurriedly packed the remains of their lunch. But just before they departed, they overheard one crow asking another if she knew the answer to the riddle. The couple waited with bated breath, and indeed, the crow claimed to know the solution. After the dragon's death, this crow had sneaked into the queen's bedchambers hoping to feast on his remains. With her own eyes she had seen what the queen had done with the dismembered dragon. She had paid the tanner one thousand silver coins to skin the dragon; she then gave the royal seamstress one hundred silver coins to sew the skin into a pillowcase on which the queen could rest her head. The dragon's bones were saved as well and carved into hairpins to adorn the queen's hair.

The old couple did not quite understand the meaning of what they had heard, but they knew that their son was in grave danger, so they hastened to the palace in Tagaung. Pauk Kyaing was overjoyed to see his parents, but their happy reunion soon took a sad turn as he described his miserable plight. When his parents recounted the birds' conversation, however, Pauk Kyaing realized that the crow's explanation must be the solution to the riddle.

For the first time in many nights he fell back into a deep and restful sleep. When the queen came before him the next morning, she was dismayed and chagrined to find that Pauk Kyaing could answer her riddle. To dispel all doubt, the king presented both the pillowcase made from the *naga*'s skin and the hairpins made from his bones as proof. Realizing that her plan for revenge had failed, the queen prepared herself for her execution. Having recently wrestled with the disturbing prospect of his own death, the king, whose heart was truly magnanimous, pardoned the queen a second time.

The advice Pauk Kyaing had received as a farewell gift from his teacher had shown him the way and enabled him to become king. During his long and blessed rule, Pauk Kyaing always followed this advice. The kingdom grew and prospered under his wise and capable rule, and he was known by all as a clever and wise monarch. In the end the king and the queen bore two blind boys who founded yet another legendary kingdom in Burma.

The Omen

Long ago there were two brothers of royal birth named Thamala and Vimala. Thamala, the older of the two, eventually became king while his younger brother was the crown prince.

King Thamala reigned over the region's fertile plains, where many of his subjects worked the fields or kept livestock. Among the many homesteads there was one particular little piece of land where a husband and wife raised vegetables. The pumpkin was their finest crop: a luminous golden squash that contrasted sharply with the profuse green leaves that hung from the plants' thick and elegantly intertwining vines. The couple also had a daughter who was not only good-natured but also so extraordinarily beautiful that no one who passed could fail to notice her, whether she was tending the fields with her parents or helping to bring in the bountiful harvest. Her flawless skin shimmered almost ethereally, as if reflecting the golden luster of the pumpkins.

As harvest time neared, King Thamala determined that it was time for him not only to choose a bride but also to send out his troops to get a better understanding of his kingdom. The soldiers received explicit instructions to keep an eye out for young women whose notable virtues might qualify them to be his future spouse. As the men inspected the far-flung regions of the realm in fulfillment of their duties, they eventually came to the little farm with the abundant vegetable harvests. When the farmer's daughter caught sight of the approaching soldiers, she was afraid and ran into the pumpkin patch to hide. But her radiant beauty could not be concealed, and the men soon discovered her amid the thick foliage. Although they had already been combing the rural districts for a considerable time, they had never come across a girl who could compare in appearance with the farmer's daughter.

Her exquisite beauty was plain to see, despite her simple clothing and the mud splatters she had picked up in her mad dash through the pumpkin patch. Convinced that the king would be delighted with this enchanting candidate, the soldiers pulled her out of the tangled leaves and vegetables where she had sought refuge. They then returned in all haste to the palace in order to present to the king the beautiful young woman they had rooted out of her peculiar hiding place.

The king was indeed deeply impressed by the young woman his soldiers had spied among the pumpkin vines, and he made her his wife. People endearingly called her the Pumpkin Queen, an allusion both to her background and to the circumstances of her discovery. Not long thereafter a son was born to the royal couple. People rejoiced throughout the kingdom, and yet there was one person who found in this no cause to celebrate: the crown prince. Desiring to be king himself, Vimala could not tolerate the birth of a direct heir whose claim to the throne would be stronger than his own.

Being of no mind to be displaced, Vimala instigated a revolt against his older brother. Within a short time the king was slain in battle, and the crown prince ascended to the throne. To ensure that no one else could lay claim to power, he banished his sister-in-law and her young son without any advance warning to a distant location in the border region between the Karen and the Mon.

So abrupt was the queen's departure that her court was unable to make appropriate preparations, and the laborious journey ended tragically for mother and child. The unfortunate queen eventually grew so exhausted that her milk failed. Hoping desperately that someone would find him and care for him, she wrapped her son snugly in blankets and laid him by the side of the road.

Aside from various animals, many of them dangerous, there were few inhabitants of this border region. Among those few was a widow who tended a herd of buffalo and who was known by the name Mi Nankarai. One morning as she was wandering through the hills, she discovered, to her amazement, an infant wailing bitterly in the tall grass. Because this was a favored grazing ground for the buffalo, and because the child lay right in the path of the approaching beasts, she put a quick halt to the animals' progress, lest the child be trodden beneath their hooves. The cloths in which the child was wrapped seemed to the buffalo herder inconceivably precious. Mi Nankarai surmised that the boy had been abandoned by some noble house, perhaps even a house of royal lineage. Because she had found him so near the border that separated the Karen and the Mon, she named him Kwan Eet Thar, which in the language of the Mon meant something like "Prince of the Border."

Although she scarcely had the means to raise a child, the widow took the wailing infant into her care without a second thought. She nourished him on buffalo milk from her herd and gradually the weakened foundling regained his strength. In the end he grew into a healthy boy who followed his foster mother's every step as she led her herd through the trackless border territories. From daily experience and observation he learned not only how to care for the animals in his charge, but also to appreciate the countless wonders of nature. As the boy developed into a young man, Nankarai encouraged him to master the martial arts just as her Karen and Mon forefathers had done. The years of wandering across jagged terrain with the herd had shaped and toughened the boy's body and mind. It was no surprise, then, when he proved to be an extraordinarily gifted and disciplined student who readily mastered the basics and showed a special talent for the traditional art of Burmese boxing known as Lethwei. This particular type of fighting was one of the most important for single combat, and was practiced by nearly all men regardless of their heritage or social class.

As soon as he had mastered the various fighting techniques, the young man returned to his foster mother in the countryside, where he resumed the more peaceful occupation of tending the herd. As Nankarai grew older, the physical strain of scrambling across the rocky landscape began to take its toll. She was finding it increasingly difficult to tend the animals. Kwan Eet Thar assumed responsibility for the herd so that his foster mother could stay home and rest.

The young man enjoyed his work as a herder wandering lazily alongside the buffalo through the soft hillsides. One day as he strode along, Kwan Eet Thar met a hunter who had lately come from the palace, where he had heard rumors that he now shared with the young herdsman. A group of rabble-rousers was preparing an insurrection in hopes of forcing King Vimala to abdicate. The man pulling the strings and stoking the flames went by the name "Lumbar," which meant something like "giant," because by all accounts he was well over six feet tall. The hunter reported that Lumbar and his band would soon be arriving in seven large ships in order to declare war on the king. Kwan Eet Thar listened enthralled, for it was seldom he met anyone at all while tending the herd, never mind someone with tidings of an impending palace revolt. The young man begged the hunter to take him along so that he might do his part defending the palace and the realm. He asserted that he had attained mastery in the martial arts and that he was therefore prepared to be the king's champion in single combat against the giant. The hunter eyed this youth on the brink of manhood and could see for himself that he was in outstanding physical condition, well built and brimming with vigor.

When they parted ways the hunter promised to deliver the young man's offer to the king. When he reached the palace he described his encounter with the young herdsman, remarking on his obvious strength, his presumed abilities, and his readiness to defend the king against the overgrown marauder. The king, filled with dread by the impending confrontation, accepted the hunter's offer to bring the young man to the palace.

Upon his arrival, everyone was duly impressed by Kwan Eet Thar's bearing and his obvious physical strength. The king was grateful that the young herdsman was eager to accept the challenge to fight the giant. In return he offered him the hand of his daughter and so also the prospect, as crown prince, of being next in line for the throne. Being loath to commit to an undertaking of such consequence without consulting his foster mother, Kwan Eet Thar asked for some time to think it over and for permission to visit her.

The king consented, and upon his return to the borderlands between the Karen and the Mon, Kwan Eet Thar told his foster mother all that had transpired. Nankarai listened closely and encouraged him to return to the palace and accept the challenge. After giving him her blessing, she offered him one more piece of important advice for the road: Knowing that the hulking figure would have the advantage in a hand-to-hand contest, she recommended the following trick. If he found himself in trouble, Kwan Eet Thar should cry out: "Here comes your mother!" As soon as his opponent turned to look whether it was true, he must topple him with his spear. Reflecting on Nankarai's parting words, Kwan Eet Thar set off on the long journey back to the palace.

When he arrived he found his opponent already waiting impatiently for him. The giant was truly of unprecedented stature. His limbs appeared to have no end, and his head was perched so high that it seemed to block the sun. A man of lesser honor and resolve might have had grave misgivings about going toe-to-toe with this human colossus. Not so Kwan Eet Thar, who immediately prepared for battle. A bitter struggle ensued. Despite the difference in size Kwan Eet Thar proved to be a worthy opponent, even after several skirmishes when both parties were starting to show signs of weariness. In the heat of the battle, as a last resort, Kwan Eet Thar deployed his foster mother's ruse. His cry, "Here comes your mother," had the exact effect that Nankarai had foreseen, and he seized on the momentary distraction to vanquish his foe. The throne was safe, and the grateful king, as promised, gave him his daughter's hand and promoted him to crown prince.

On the occasion of the wedding, Kwan Eet Thar's foster mother revealed to him how she had found him long ago in the borderlands, wrapped in fine vestments the like of which were seldom seen in her remote corner of the land. When the king got wind of this story he recognized at once that his daughter's husband was none other than the infant nephew he had banished from the realm along with his mother.

The king realized straightaway that this was no mere chance: Kwan Eet Thar's return and triumphant defense of the kingdom were a clear omen. And so Vimala immediately handed over power to the rightful heir to the throne.

How to Spell "Buffalo"

It happened at a time when the newly founded kingdom of Ava was in an uproar. The king was deeply concerned about the conditions in the country; strife and dissension were flaring up everywhere. In many places even the teachings of the Buddha seemed no longer to hold sway. Therefore the king sent his monks out to all the villages to listen to the people and urge them not to forget the words of the Enlightened One.

One of these monks and his escorts arrived in a village in the northeast, near the border with China. The people there greeted him kindly, but were quick to tell him that they considered his presence unnecessary. In their village the religious duties had never been neglected; the monastery had always been in the hands of capable monks and abbots. Thus the villagers received this missionary from the distant capital with respect, but also with a certain reticence.

Finally, they came to the visitor with a question. "We do not believe that you are as learned and pious as our abbot, Your Honor," they said to the monk. "Would you be willing to settle this question in a religious debate?"

The monk agreed and the villagers made preparations for the competition. The plan was for the scholars to ask each other questions about their religion. The opponent would have one minute to answer. Whoever exceeded the allotted time or failed to give a satisfactory answer would be the loser.

When the appointed day came, the villagers led their visitor into a specially prepared hall. The abbot was ceremoniously ushered in and the spectators cheered. They sat face-to-face on two ornate chairs adorned with velvet and gold. The village chief sounded a loud gong, and in the solemn silence that followed he said: "Let the dispute between our abbot and the monk from the royal city begin! The host will ask the first question."

The king's delegate leaned back in his chair tensely and waited with furrowed brow for a difficult first question. After a short silence the abbot leaned forward and said in a loud voice: "How do you spell the word 'buffalo'?"

Surprised and speechless, the monk shook his head. Were these people really expecting an answer to such an elemental, ridiculously simple question? He could not believe it. He stared at the abbot, expecting an explanation or a further question, but the man across from him remained silent. His gaze wandered over to his escorts from Ava, but they looked just as surprised.

The monk smiled and cleared his throat as he racked his brain in search of a clever answer to this stupid question. Just as he finally started to speak, the chief's gong rang out. The allotted time had expired, he announced. He declared the abbot the winner.

While the villagers boisterously celebrated their victory and carried the abbot back to his monastery, the monk and his companions left the village, unsure what to tell the king.

The Tale of Two Merchants

Long, long ago a poor old woman lived with her granddaughter in a little house beside a river on the outskirts of a village. The family had once been very well-off and had been counted among the most respected members of the community, but those days were long past. Apart from a few shabby pieces of furniture, the house was now bare. At night the wind whistled through the drafty walls, and their kitchen was little more than an old rusty pot over a makeshift fireplace. A bronze cup was their only possession of any value, but they did not appreciate just how precious it truly was. To the old woman and her granddaughter it was just another cup.

One day two peddlers came across the river to sell cheap baubles in the village. The first merchant came to the house and gradually brought out necklaces, earrings, bracelets, and more. He spoke glowingly of his wares, and the young girl was soon enraptured. Oh, how they glittered and sparkled! She had seen some of the other girls with necklaces like these, and she asked her grandmother to buy something for her. Sadly the grandmother confessed that they had no money and nothing of value that they might offer as payment.

At that moment the peddler spotted the bronze cup. He asked to see it and examined it thoroughly in order to assess its value. This merchant was very greedy, and though he wanted the cup, he did not wish to trade fairly for it, so he threw it carelessly into the mud and claimed that it was worthless. Privately he was hoping that the two would leave it lying there, where he might snatch it up on a second round through the village. Then he packed up his jewelry and left.

The two women were puzzled. Had the stranger not asked explicitly to examine the cup? Why would he leave it lying in the mud? They picked it up, confused and thinking they might ask for a second opinion.

Shortly thereafter the second merchant paid a call to the grandmother and granddaughter, and they showed him the piece in question. Now, this merchant was an upright and honest man. After examining the cup he declared that it was a remarkable object worth more than all of his jewelry together. He polished a corner of the dull metal and the women marveled at its radiance.

What joy this news brought to the granddaughter! The grandmother praised the man's integrity, and in the end they traded the cup for all the man's trinkets. Both sides took satisfaction from the exchange. The peddler packed up his cup, got back into his boat, and made for the other side. The first, deceitful merchant rounded the corner just in time to see the honest peddler going ashore with his new possession, and he turned pale with envy.

The White Crow and Love

High at the top of a mountain near Bagan lived a young woman named Zanthi. She was actually a *naga* princess, a descendent from a malicious family of dragon-like serpent beings who lived in a distant underground kingdom. There she had grown tired of the ruthless and lawless life of the *naga*, and desired a more virtuous existence. Time and again she had begged her father for permission to leave the underworld to join the world of men in human form. In the end she managed to convince her father of the seriousness of her intentions, and he let her go her way in peace. Zanthi settled at the top of a high mountain surrounded by an abundance of unspoiled nature.

In her new home the princess would rise each morning at dawn as soon as the first rays of sunlight fell across the ragged contours of the mountains. She would immediately begin her meditation exercises, to which she devoted a considerable part of her day.

One day, as she was deeply immersed in contemplative thought, she was suddenly torn from her reveries by a deafening noise that thundered up from the forest around the lower slopes of the mountain. Having spent so much time alone in the wild, Zanthi had grown familiar with the behaviors and habits of the other animals that called the mountain home and could recognize each and every species by its individual language. She also knew the sound of the wind in the trees and many other natural phenomena, but the present din was nothing of the sort. Who or what was behind this dreadful clamor? It sounded like the pounding hooves of a great number of horses breaking through the undergrowth as they passed through the forest. The rhythm and gait suggested that it was by no means a wild herd, but rather a mounted guard of some kind. The thought made her uneasy.

But as the horses and riders emerged from the trees her apprehension vanished. At the front of the pack rode a handsome young prince with sun-kissed skin and a kind face. Zanthi knew immediately that she had nothing to fear. As the troops approached, the prince spied the lovely princess staring intently down at him from her rocky ledge. He had never before encountered a woman of such exquisite beauty; even the splendor of the pristine natural world that surrounded her paled in comparison. The young leader, mesmerized, called an immediate halt and ordered his troops to pitch their tents and rest. He would not for any price let slip the chance to pass some time with this enchanting mountain dweller. For several blissful days the prince and Zanthi were inseparable. Eventually, despite the pleasure of her company and the unexpectedly deep feelings he felt for her, he knew that he would soon have to leave this gentle beauty. He could not forever neglect his responsibilities to the people and the royal household. But before he bid her a reluctant farewell, the prince swore to his beloved Zanthi that he would be forever faithful to her. He swore to bring her to the royal palace as soon as he was able so they could be united once and for all.

Zanthi watched with a heavy heart as the men broke camp, mounted their horses, and set off on the long ride down to the valley, led by her beloved prince. But she took solace in his declaration of love and the promise he made before his departure. She did not take her eyes off the troops for a moment as they made their way over the rocky terrain, not until the forest once again swallowed them up and took them away from her. Even then she lingered awhile at her post on the edge of the cliff, listening to the sounds of the riders as they tramped through the underbrush. Zanthi was sure that her prince would soon be sending for her.

As the days passed without a single word from him she began to worry. Perhaps he had met with some misfortune on his journey to the palace. As the days turned to weeks and the weeks to months, the princess became increasingly discouraged. In the meantime she had discovered that she was carrying the Sun Prince's child, and as her time drew nearer and she had still not heard from him she asked a bird to bring the prince the message that she would soon bring his child into the world. From all the many feathered beasts of the mountain she chose as messenger the white crow, for she would be visible by day or night. Her feathers would both shimmer in the sunlight and glow in the soft glimmer of the moon as she flew through the sky on her important mission. Zanthi instructed the crow to return only after she was sure that the prince had received her message.

With the note tightly in her grasp the crow soared out over the mountains. She could see the mighty Irrawaddy far below her and set her course by following the bends in the river. Soon she reached the foothills that surrounded the prince's royal palace, and it was not long before the residents of the castle noticed the unfamiliar bird sitting on the palace wall clutching a scroll. They lured her down from the rampart and took her to the prince. As he read the message he was instantly transported back to the blissful time he had spent with the beautiful mountain princess.

His numerous duties and pursuits had kept the prince from sending for her as he had promised, and after a few months had passed, the memories of their time together began to fade. But this message about the impending birth of his child caused all the feelings of happiness and love that he had felt in Zanthi's presence to come flooding back. The prince regretted deeply that his day-to-day duties had driven his promise from his mind. In order to alleviate his guilt and to express his utter happiness at receiving her message, the prince selected his most valuable ruby ring, a crimson glittering stone, as a symbol of his deep love for the beautiful princess. He wrapped the ring carefully in a soft silk handkerchief and asked the crow to deliver it to the princess for him.

The crow set off on the long journey home to the mountains with the precious package. But no sooner had she left the palace behind than she noticed a harbor where merchants and sailors from all the different regions of the country had apparently gathered to buy goods, sell their wares, and barter.

Knowing that she had a long and difficult flight ahead of her, the crow thought it might be wise to find a bit of nourishment. She spotted a group of merchants sitting together lustily eating and drinking and thought she might be able to nick some scraps from their sumptuous meal. The packet with the ring made it hard to hop around collecting tidbits, so she deposited it at the foot of a nearby tree where she could keep an eye on it and reach it quickly when she was ready to head home. Under the table where the merchants boisterously ate and conversed lay morsels of every imaginable delicacy. For the crow, this was a marvelous feast and she soon became so swept up in the delights of the meal that she completely forgot about the treasure that lay only a few steps away. Meanwhile, one of the merchants, passing by the tree, happened to spy the carefully wrapped package. Curious what it might contain, he opened it and looked inside.

The merchant was unprepared for the brilliance of the color that struck his eye. The deep red stone radiated a fire matched only by the power of true love itself. The ruby's splendor entranced him and he knew at once that the ring must be priceless. Since it seemed no one was guarding the treasure, the merchant could not resist slipping the jewel into his pocket. Knowing well that the owner could return at any moment to claim the package, he concealed the theft by replacing the ring with a small piece of dung of similar size and weight, which he carefully rewrapped in the soft silk handkerchief.

The crow, now fortified by the treats from the traders' banquet table, returned to the tree where she had left the valuable parcel. She picked it up, flew back to the mountaintop by the fastest route possible, and presented it to Zanthi. Though it had been months since the princess had heard from the prince, still she secretly hoped that there was some compelling explanation for his silence and that her love for him was mutual. With trembling fingers she opened the prince's beautiful silken package, expecting a letter. But when she found the dung inside, the message could not have been clearer. In that instant the last spark of hope was extinguished. There would be no happy reunion with her beloved prince. Zanthi's heart was broken, and even the natural beauty of the mountain landscape had lost its charm. Renouncing the earthly realm, she cast off her alluring human shell, which had brought nothing but pain and sorrow, and once again she assumed her original form as a *naga* princess. Before she returned to her father's kingdom in the underworld, she crawled to a nearby cave and there in the shade of a tree, just inside the entrance, she laid three eggs. Thus freed from the last remnants of her earthly entanglements, she bid farewell once and for all to her former mountain paradise and descended again into the kingdom of the *nagas*.

Not long thereafter a hunter came up the mountain in search of game. It was scorching hot, and the climb was strenuous, so he kept an eye out for a place to rest. The long shadow cast by the tree near the entrance to the cave caught his eye, and he decided to pause there and catch his breath. After he had recovered he took a look around and noticed a strange sparkling from inside the cave. Thinking he had perhaps stumbled upon a hidden treasure trove, he was eager to investigate. But instead of gold and jewels, he discovered three eggs, each one more unusual than the last. One was such a dark brown color it looked as if it were made of polished ebony. The second shone as white as the foam on the waves as they crash upon the shore. The third glistened as if made of pure gold. Although the treasure was not exactly what he had hoped for, the hunter knew he had made an extraordinary find. Not knowing whether the owner of the eggs was nearby, he quickly padded them with moss, stuffed them into his knapsack, and set out back down the mountain without a moment's delay.

The route to the hunter's home led over crags and uneven paths, not the ideal course for someone carrying such a fragile cargo. Then the inevitable happened: The hunter slipped on a wet stone and fell. The golden egg broke. Rubies and numerous other kinds of jewels spilled out of the shell, and for an instant the ground surrounding the place where the egg had split open was covered with glittering precious stones that shot gleaming colors into the sky. The fireworks were short-lived, however, for the heavy jewels quickly sank deep into the soft earth.

Disappointed, the hunter stopped to rest at the edge of a lake, where he was surprised by a sudden storm. The rivers overran their banks and the two remaining eggs were washed away by the rushing current of the Irrawaddy. The dark brown egg magically made its way to Thandwe, where it lay undamaged on the riverbank until a beautiful human child hatched out of it: a princess, who would one day become the ruler of this land. The shining white egg was carried by the river all the way to Nyaung-U, where the sandbanks cushioned it and kept the fragile shell from breaking. There, an elderly farmer and his wife, who were that day combing the beach for valuable items, discovered the shimmering object at the edge of the water. The two old people knew at once that this was no ordinary egg. They picked it up with great care and decided to consult with a hermit they knew who was highly regarded for his wisdom and virtue. Perhaps he could clarify the meaning of this find.

The hermit noted the unusual glow that emanated from the egg and warned the couple to take especially good care of the treasure that good fortune had bestowed upon them. He predicted that one day a boy with a noble disposition and a glorious future would emerge from this egg. The two old ones, who had never had children of their own, were overjoyed at the hermit's prophecy, and they kept a sharp eye on the egg. One day the first cracks began to appear in its shell and it was not long before a little, perfectly formed boy emerged. His skin had a glow about it that was similar to the shell of the egg out of which he came. It was obvious that the prophecy of the hermit had come true when the boy exhibited extraordinary wisdom, grace, and other traits unusual in one so young. The couple, wanting to give the boy every possible advantage, taught him all they knew about nature, the changing seasons, and the best time to plant and harvest crops. They also taught him how important it was to treat others with respect and empathy. When Pyusawhti was old enough to begin a formal education, the pair entrusted him to a highly regarded monk. The monk was very pleased with his exceptional pupil, who proved to be knowledgeable and gifted in all fields. The teaching in the monastery was extensive, with a focus on religious instruction and martial arts. It is said that Pyusawhti developed a taste for competitive sports and became a master of the art of archery.

While Pyusawhti was receiving his education, his biological father had ascended to the throne. Even as king he was still filled with sorrow for failing to reunite with the beautiful mountain princess and for never getting to know his child. He had searched far and wide for both of them for many years, but his efforts had been in vain. His despair and the extent to which he blamed himself for what had happened were so great and palpable that even the spirits felt sorry for the dejected ruler. And so he learned of the crow's detour during her flight back home, the related theft of the ruby ring and the subsequent replacement with the dung. As punishment for her negligence, the king, who was descended from the sun and was able to unleash its power, scorched the crow's plumage. Ever since then, crows have not been white but black as coal.

The spirits showed the king the way to the small settlement of Nyaung-U. The king was overjoyed to find his well-raised son there, and he never tired of telling the boy about his history and his mother. He still deeply regretted breaking his promise to the princess, for he realized that Zanthi had renounced the world thinking he had betrayed her. Together, father and son honored her memory by bringing an offering of milk and flowers to one of the nearby *naga* caves.

To this day, couples in Burma who want a son try to earn the good graces of the *naga*s with similar sacrifices.

Mu Yeh Peh and the Wages of Love

There was a time in the history of Burma when the Shan people ruled a large part of the country, including a small Karen village where a young woman named Mu Yeh Peh lived. She was renowned far and wide for her beauty, but beyond that she also had an extraordinary gift—any time she drank water it would immediately radiate in bright and lovely golden beams from her face and throat.

Word of this seemingly supernatural phenomenon traveled quickly, and soon even the

Shan king had heard of it. It was customary for kings at that time to take several of the most beautiful and extraordinary women in the kingdom as their wives. The king's curiosity was aroused, and he set off at once with his retinue for Mu Yeh Peh's village.

News of the king's approaching visit spread like wildfire, and Mu Yeh Peh found herself confronted with an impossible dilemma: She was already in love with a young man she wanted to marry. What is more, the Karen were forbidden to marry outside their tribe. The restriction applied all the more to Mu Yeh Peh, who, because of her beauty and special power, was so revered by all Karen people that she had become a symbol of hope for the tribe. So the Karen resolved at once to cover her in a veil and hide her in the mountains. The king arrived shortly thereafter. He was furious when he learned that his bride was not there and no one could tell him where she was or when she might return. Did they mean to say he had come all this way for nothing? He sentenced the Karen to hard labor until Mu Yeh Peh should appear.

Yet even under the yoke of this punishment, not a single Karen betrayed the young beauty. Meanwhile, the king sulked in his palace, his wrath increasing with each passing day. In the end he proclaimed that all Karen women must henceforth lug heavy lumber to the palace every day, where they would then be forced to drink. Hopefully Mu Yeh Peh would thus be exposed.

Instead, the Karen simply hid her deeper in the mountains. But when she caught wind of the way the king was tormenting the women of her tribe, she was plagued by doubts. Should she not turn herself in? She would refuse the king's offer of marriage, and then?...Presumably a death sentence.

For one whole day and night Mu Yeh Peh wrestled with uncertainty, and then she made up her mind. She had no choice; she must surrender and release her tribe from their suffering.

Mu Yeh Peh mingled with the other women as they struggled along to the palace laden with heavy lumber. There she lined up for the obligatory drink. She took a sip before the very eyes of the royal guard, and she was instantly revealed by the golden glow. They led her directly to the king, who straightaway asked her to marry him. She refused politely but firmly and begged for lenience. But the king knew no mercy and had her thrown into the dungeon. She spent a few days locked up, sick with longing for her beloved and lamenting her lot, before the soldiers came to fetch her. Any lingering hopes she might have had were quickly dispelled. The guards led her to a large open square before the palace. They had dug a deep hole there, and they pushed Mu Yeh Peh into it. The indignant king presided over the proceedings and then gave the order: Two elephants began rolling a large tree trunk in the direction of the pit. The tree trunk was meant to seal Mu Yeh Peh in her grave, but when the elephants saw her they refused to entomb her.

The king boiled with rage. He ordered that blind elephants be brought, and so it was done. The soldiers could barely contain the crowd as the execution resumed.

The animals slowly approached the pit. Suddenly Mu Yeh Peh's beloved, the best climber far and wide, shinnied up a tall bamboo trunk so that it leaned ever lower in the direction of the ditch. He was hoping to scoop up his beloved and escape with her!

But the bamboo was too short. The young man could not reach Mu Yeh Peh, and instead of helping her get away, he got himself captured and thrown into the pit alongside her.

The elephants rolled the tree trunks into place until the ditch was sealed forever. Mu Yeh Peh and her beloved died together in a tender embrace.

To this day many Karen await the rebirth of Mu Yeh Peh in the hope that she will unite her tribe and lead them to a better future.

The Beautiful Woman and the Lazy Dimwit

The wealthy rice merchant's villa was splendidly decorated. The aroma of delicious curries, fragrantly roasted fish, and fresh fruit wafted through the halls. The day had come on which his only daughter, a young woman known throughout the whole city for her beauty, was to be married. The groom also came from a wealthy family, and, as such, the rice merchant was certain that nothing stood in the way of this couple's happy future.

After the wedding, the merchant had a palace built for the young couple. It was trimmed with gold inside and out. He made sure that they wanted for nothing. Yet after a while the son-in-law began to feel restless. He craved adventure and yearned to go out into the world, to stand on his own two feet and not to rely on his parents' or in-laws' money.

"But we have everything we need to be happy right here! Don't go!" his wife pleaded. "Our parents will support us and our children. Why expose yourself to the dangers of a long voyage?"

"I want don't want to live off someone else's back," her husband replied. "I want to be my own master and explore the world."

His wife's parents implored him to reconsider. He had a beautiful wife and a small palace. Why risk a perilous journey to faraway lands?

But the young man stood by his decision. He purchased a ship and set sail. He left behind a deeply disappointed and aggrieved wife who now wanted revenge. Since my husband does not respect my wishes, she thought to herself, I will not respect his. He is off seeking adventure, so I, too, will have some fun of my own. He despises my parents' money? Let's see how far that gets him!

She ordered her servants to find the laziest dimwit in the land and bring him to her.

To her surprise, that very evening a handsome young man was brought before her. She invited him to stay and in the darkness of the night they began to play secret love games, which became more and more passionate as the weeks went by. Months passed and one day the loafer asked his lover what was going to happen if her husband returned? That question had not yet even crossed her mind, so together they came up with a cunning plot. The following night they went to the graveyard and dug up the body of a recently deceased young woman. They dragged it back to the palace, laid it in the marriage bed, set the palace on fire, and fled to another province.

The hungry flames burned the house down to the foundation, and in the ruins the parents discovered the charred remains of a woman. Their hearts were sick with grief and their wits confused.

The daughter had taken all of her jewelry and gems with her and at first was able to live magnificently on these riches. But because her lover was genuinely lazy and because she herself did not know the first thing about work, her funds were soon depleted.

"So, what are we going to do when all the money is gone?" asked the loafer, who had quite literally grown fat off their sweet life of luxury. The woman had no immediate answer to this question. It took her a whole day and night to come up with her next plan. "You have become so large," she explained, "no one in our city will be able to recognize you. I look pretty much unchanged and when my parents see me they will think I am their dead daughter's doppelgänger and they will take us in."

The two traveled back to their hometown and sat by the side of the road near the rice merchant's villa dressed as beggars. They had only been there a few hours when the mother came along. Upon seeing her daughter she cried out: "My eyes must be playing tricks on me! You are the spitting image of our deceased child!"

"We are only poor beggars and ask only for a small pittance," answered the daughter, disguising her voice.

"Oh no, you are a gift! Follow me to our house. You are to be pampered. You will want for nothing."

They were both given fine clothes and food, and the rice merchant and his wife, in their sadness, invited them to stay. The sight of a person who so closely resembled their child greatly comforted them. They rebuilt the burned-down palace stone for stone and asked the alleged beggars to make themselves at home there.

Time passed and one day a grand merchant vessel sailed into the harbor. It was laden with gold, gems, fine cloth, and exotic spices. It was the husband who, happy to be back, immediately set out for the home of his wife's parents. When he learned about the fire and the gruesome death of his wife his heart was broken. Plagued by sadness, guilt, and self-blame, he wandered the city streets aimlessly. All the greater was his surprise when he suddenly stood in front of a palace that looked every bit the twin of the one that had burned down. He went inside, roaming through the hallways until he finally reached the bedroom where he found his wife in the arms of her lover.

"You are mistaking me for someone else," she proclaimed. "I am not your wife but simply a beggar."

Her parents rushed over, as did the neighbors, all testifying to having witnessed the devastating fire and the discovery of the charred corpse with their own eyes.

The husband would not be duped. "Since my departure I have yearned desperately for my beloved wife. Do you really think I wouldn't recognize her?"

Each side claimed to know the truth, and no one was able to offer up a solution, so they found the highest judge in the land to listen to their case and give her verdict.

She listened to the different versions of the story and then asked everyone to leave the room. She wanted to speak privately with each of the parties.

When she was alone with the husband, she said, "Everyone's testimony and all the evidence speaks against you. If you are telling the truth, you are trying to get back a woman who is deceiving you and lying shamelessly. That is unforgivable. If you are lying, you are trying to take another man's wife. That, too, is unforgivable. Why do not you just take me as your wife? I am not married, I am very respectable, and I am certainly not ugly."

"Your Honor," the man replied, "with all due respect, your offer is appealing, but I know that you are only trying to tempt me. I am married. This purported beggar woman is my wife and the one I love and the one I left against her will in order to go on some silly adventure."

The judge sent him out and called in the loafer.

"My dear," she began in a friendly voice, "you don't seem like the type who frets about things. Why do you covet another man's wife? Take me instead. I have money, live alone, and would be happy to have a man. We could live a life of luxury together."

"Splendid!" answered the delighted dimwit. "One woman is as good as the next."

The judge sent him out and asked to speak to the woman who professed to be a beggar.

"Goodness sakes, I don't understand you. Why would you want to stay with that loafer when you could be the wife of this respected and rich explorer?"

"Your Honor," the woman explained, "you are a woman. I am a woman. We both know that we are fruit.

While the fruit hangs in the tree it belongs to that tree, but as soon as it falls to the ground, it can no longer return to its tree."

The judge shook her head and ordered everyone back into the room to give her verdict: "This woman," she began, "belongs to the returned sailor. The loafer has committed adultery and is thus obligated to pay compensation. But what does this good-for-nothing have to offer? He doesn't have a cent to his name. No livestock. No property."

To the purported beggar woman she declared: "Fruit cannot return to the tree, but a daughter can return to her mother."

Finally, she turned to the husband: "Your fruit is rotten. If you insist, I will let you have it. But if you want my advice: Take your ship, sail far away, and find someone else to love!"

The Fisherman's Reward

The fishermen had pulled their boats ashore and lashed them firmly to the palm trees. They could tell by the colors of the sea and sky that a heavy storm was brewing and they must take every precaution.

Just then a messenger galloped in from the palace demanding fresh fish. The king insisted on having at least one fried fish at every meal, and the palace scullery was clean out. When the messenger saw that the fishermen's baskets were also empty, beads of sweat dotted his brow. His Majesty did not take kindly to unfulfilled wishes, least of all when it came to his favorite foods. The servant asked the fishermen to row back out, but they pointed to the deep black clouds and the white-caps frothing along the crests of the growing waves. None of them felt inclined to risk his life. The envoy pleaded with them—they had no idea what would happen to him if he returned to the court empty-handed! At last a brave young fisherman took pity on him and declared that he was willing to take the risk.

Together they launched his boat into the crashing surf. He rowed for all he was worth, and it was not long before he was all but lost to view down inside the deep troughs of the waves.

The storm's ferocity increased. It started to rain, and gradually the fishermen started to think that the sea had swallowed their comrade forever. Hours passed. The servant of the court was on the brink of despair when an especially large breaker suddenly spilled the rowboat back ashore. And there sat the fisherman with a big, fat fish in his hands.

The fisherman and the envoy raced to the palace, where the fisherman was led immediately to the king's apartments. Outside the very last door the chamberlain was waiting for him. He gazed at the fish. "You have made a fine catch," he remarked pointedly. "But whatever reward you get, half belongs to me."

"I risked my life in the storm," the shocked fisherman protested. "I'll give you a tenth."

"No. Fifty-fifty or you'll not get past this door."

"That's completely unfair," cried the outraged fisherman. "Why should you get anything at all?"

"Because if you don't see the king then you'll get nothing at all. Simple as that."

The fisherman realized that he was powerless, and he agreed to the terms.

The chamberlain opened the heavy door and announced the arrival of a fisherman with fresh fish.

At the sight of the fish the king's mouth began to water. The chef prepared it quickly, and in no time at all the king was lost in the flavors of his favorite dish. When he was utterly satisfied, he reclined on his cushions and summoned the fisherman.

"You have earned my gratitude. What do you desire? How can I demonstrate my appreciation? Gems? A new boat?"

The fisherman looked at the floor and shook his head. "No, Your Highness, nothing of the kind. I want only twenty lashes across my bare back."

The king burst out laughing. "I see you are no stranger to a jest. How delightful! But speak truthfully; you may name your reward. Your word is my command."

The fisherman stood by his original request, and so the reluctant king called for a whip.

The young man bared his back, and the king struck him as softly as he could.

"My Lord, not so timidly. Give it all you've got."

Not wanting to break his promise, the king laid into the fisherman with all his might. After the tenth stroke, the fisherman jumped up and cried, "Stop, that's enough. Now it's the chamberlain's turn."

The confused king turned to the servant, who had followed the proceedings without a word, his face white as chalk.

Stammering, the chamberlain confessed to the arrangement he had imposed on the fisherman, whereupon he received his own ten lashes.

When it was done, the king relieved the chamberlain of the powers he had abused and appointed the bold fisherman to take his place.

The Best Storyteller

In a certain village there lived four young men who had been close friends since early childhood. After a long day's work in the fields, they liked to meet at a teahouse and exchange the most marvelous tales. They would often sit together until late in the evening trying to outdo one another to see which of them was the best storyteller.

One day they noticed a stranger eating noodle soup at a nearby table. He wore an elegant longyi, a handsome shirt, and on top of that an exquisite vest. The four friends put their heads together and came up with a plan to trick the traveler out of his fancy clothes.

A short time later they sidled up to the stranger and started a conversation. They asked where he was from and where the road might be taking him. Eventually they suggested a competition. Each of them should give an earnest account of a ludicrous story. If anyone betrayed even the slightest skepticism, that person would become a slave to the others. The proprietor of the teahouse would be the referee.

The stranger thought it was a good suggestion and agreed to participate. They ordered another round of tea with crackers and roasted melon seeds to nibble on. Then the first of the young men started his tale.

"My mother loved fruit, and best of all mangos. A tall, proud mango tree grew in front of our house, and when I was still in her womb she asked my father to pick a few of the delicious fruits for her. My father replied that he would be happy to do so if only the ripe mangos did not hang so high in the tree. It would be a dangerous climb. He'd gladly go to the market for her if she liked. My mother insisted on mangos from her own tree, since they were sweeter and juicier, so she asked my three brothers to pick some for her, but they, too, declared that it would be too perilous to climb the tree. My dear mother was so disappointed that I could hardly stand it. In the night I crept out of her womb and clambered up the tree. Over the next several hours I harvested nearly every mango from its branches and piled them into a neat pyramid at the foot of my mother's bed. Just before sunrise I crawled back into her belly. When she awoke she could not believe her eyes. No one knew how the mangos had gotten into her room, but now she could eat as many as she liked, and she had plenty to share with my brothers and the neighbors."

The young man sipped his tea and looked around expectantly, but the traveler just nodded in agreement.

And so the second young man began his tale.

"Not far from our house there is an old eucalyptus tree. It stands so tall that its crown is not infrequently lost in the clouds. Shortly after I was born—I could not have been more than two weeks old—I decided to explore the tree. Climbing up was more challenging than I expected, but still it was much easier than climbing back down. Halfway back to the ground I was nearly exhausted, and I was starting to worry that I would have to spend the night up there. Then I remembered that the village smith had a tall ladder. I ran to the smithy as fast as I could, borrowed the ladder, and ran back to the tree, where I safely completed my descent."

The stranger smiled, and in his face there was not the slightest sign that he doubted the tale's veracity.

The four friends looked at each other in disappointment. Now it was the third young man's turn.

"Even as a very young child I loved to wander alone through the jungle. One time—I had just turned one—I saw a hare disappear into a bush. Full of curiosity, I crawled in after it. I scrambled deeper and deeper into the thicket, until I found myself face-to-face not with a hare, but with a tiger. The tiger gazed at me with big, hungry eyes. I asked him whether he had noticed a hare running past. He shook his head, opened his mouth wide, and bared his teeth. There was no doubt that he intended to devour me. I told him to leave me in peace, but the foolish animal would not listen. He came closer and closer until I had no choice but to strike him. I guess I overdid it, because he split right in two and died on the spot."

The young man looked anxiously from one listener to the next. All of them sat in reflective silence; not a one betrayed even a trace of disbelief.

And so the fourth young man launched into his yarn.

"Let me say up front that I like to eat fish and also to catch them myself. Last year I spent a few days at the beach, where I borrowed a boat from a fisherman and rowed out to sea. But even after several hours I hadn't had a single bite. These waters were supposed to be teeming with fish, so I talked to the other fishermen, and they were all having similarly bad luck. For days they had been returning to shore empty-handed; even the best bait was no help.

"I decided to get to the bottom of it, so I jumped into the sea and dove down deep. The water was pleasantly warm and clear, but there were no fish in sight. After three days and nights I finally found the answer to the riddle. At the bottom of the sea lay a fish as big as a mountain. He hardly moved, but from time to time he would open his mouth. Whenever he did all of the fish from far and wide would disappear into it as if drawn by some magical force. I swam up to the monster and killed it with a single blow. I was hungry from all that diving, so I decided to make a dinner of that fish right then and there. I lit a fire, grilled the fish, and ate it. When I was done, I resurfaced, swam to shore, and told the other fishermen that their troubles were over and that they would soon be returning with full nets."

Confident of his victory, the narrator looked around, but everyone just nodded. No one expressed even a shred of doubt about the story's details.

Now it was the stranger's turn.

"Not long ago I owned a great many papaya trees. One of them was especially tall and shapely, but it bore no fruit. My workers recommended I cut it down, but I could not bring myself to do it. The following year it suddenly produced four large papayas more beautiful and magnificent than on any other tree. When they were ripe and glowing reddish-golden in the sun we harvested them. When I cut them open a young man stepped out of each one. From that moment on, the four of them became my slaves. Unfortunately they were lethargic and lazy, and after only a few weeks they all ran away. Since then I have scoured the land in search of them, and it looks like today is my lucky day, because I have found you at last, my runaway slaves. Pack your things and return with me to my estate."

The four young men were frozen with fear. They would not even touch their tea. If they went along with the stranger's story then they would have to follow his command and go off with him. But if they questioned his word, they would lose the competition and again be forced to serve as his slaves.

The traveler smiled broadly at them. "Well?" he asked.

When they had nothing to say, the proprietor of the teahouse wanted to know whether they believed the tale. None of the four made so much as a peep, and the proprietor declared that the traveler had won the competition.

"Since you are now my slaves," said the victor, "everything you own also belongs to me. Remove your pants and shirts and give them to me. After that I will set you free."

The four men did as they were told. The man tied their clothes into a large bundle and went on his way, singing merrily to himself as he left the village.

The Crocodile and the Monkey

A long time ago a crocodile lived on the banks of a mighty river with his wife, who often felt sick and weak. One day she told her husband that the only cure for her ailments was to eat a monkey heart. "Please, dear," she implored him, "bring me the heart of a young little monkey."

The crocodile loved his wife dearly and began his search at once. Both sides of the river were lined with tall trees, and the crocodile had often seen monkeys frolicking in their boughs. One monkey in particular had caught his eye because he was so curious and bold. He would always climb out the farthest on the limbs that hung over the river, and he clambered nimbly and fearlessly into the highest branches. Though small in stature, this little monkey clearly had a big heart. So the crocodile swam to the middle of the stream, where he kept a sharp lookout. He spent the whole day in the water and was just about to give up when he spotted the monkey in a mango tree.

"Hey, Monkey," he called, "the fruits on the other side of the river are much bigger and juicier. I'll take you over there if you like."

"A likely story," replied the monkey. "Why should the fruit be better there than here? You just want to eat me."

"Not at all! I was only trying to help," claimed the crocodile. But the little monkey would not be taken in.

This encounter repeated itself time and again over the next several days. The crocodile regaled the monkey with tales of unimaginably large bananas and mouth-watering papayas on the far bank, but the monkey was not buying it. At least not until his curiosity finally got the better of him and he accepted the crocodile's offer to ferry him over.

The monkey climbed onto the crocodile's back and off they went. About halfway across the stream the crocodile began to submerge.

"What are you doing?" cried the horrified monkey. "I'll drown!"

So the crocodile confessed that he had in fact been lying all along and that he now meant to kill the monkey for the sake of his sickly wife, who desired the monkey's heart.

The monkey laughed. "You can kill me if you like," he said, "but you won't get my heart that way. Do you really think that we monkeys carry our hearts around with us all day long? How are we supposed to spring lightly from treetop to treetop while carrying our heavy hearts?"

The crocodile needed to think about this.

"We hide our hearts in trees," the monkey went on. "We tuck them away in little hollows or in nests. If your wife is dead set on eating a monkey heart, then bring me back to shore and I'll fetch not one, but two of them right away."

The crocodile swam back to shore and let the monkey go.

The monkey returned almost immediately with two extraordinarily large and juicy figs. He insisted that they were especially strong monkey hearts, and he gave them to the crocodile, who happily brought them home to his wife. Convinced that they were monkey hearts, she ate the figs and enjoyed excellent health all the rest of her days.

The Clever Monkeys

A good long time ago there lived a man who wove and sold hats of straw. All of the farmers needed his hats to keep their heads out of the sun while they worked in the fields, so business was generally good. One day after finishing a batch of hats he packed them in a large basket and set off for the next village. It was market day there, and many people would be keen to buy his goods.

It was a strenuous hike and the sun was blazing in the blue sky, so the hat maker decided to rest awhile in the shade of a sprawling banyan tree. He intended only to catch his breath, but in the heat of the day he soon fell asleep.

When he woke some time later he could tell by the sun that he had slept a long while. Now he would have to hurry to get to the village in time. He looked around grumpily for his hats, and he could hardly believe his eyes—all of them were gone! Only the one on his head remained. The hat maker hastily searched around the massive tree, wondering what could have happened. He looked among the roots and bushes, but he did not find a single hat.

At some point he heard laughter in the tree above him. He glanced up, and in the boughs he saw a large troop of monkeys, each one with a straw hat on its head! They split their sides laughing while the hat maker cursed and threatened them and went through all kinds of contortions trying to get his hats back. The amused monkeys merely mimicked his furious gestures!

The hat maker was outraged at the way the monkeys were mocking him, but in the end it gave him an idea. The animals reminded him of ill-mannered children. Perhaps he could outsmart them.

"Oh, what a beautiful hat!" he said loudly. He took his hat in his hands, examined it from all sides, and finally put it back on his head. The monkeys imitated him.

Next the hat maker declared: "It's so hot today, isn't it?" He took his hat off again and fanned himself with it. Up in the treetop the monkeys squealed with glee and mocked him again.

A third time the man took the hat off his head and examined it critically. "Oh, I don't like this hat anymore," he said, and threw it decisively to the ground.

The monkeys laughed, took their hats in their hands, and threw them all to the ground.

Pleased with this outcome, the hat maker chuckled while the monkeys, enraged by this trick, screamed and thrashed around in the tree, but did not dare to come down. The man quickly gathered the hats and went on his way.

Many years later the hat maker's son took over his father's business. The son had children of his own, the oldest of whom decided to carry on his grandfather's trade. And so it came to pass that more than twenty years later a young man with a basket full of straw hats was making his way to the very same village, where again it was a market day.

It was still a difficult road, and again it was a hot day when the young man stopped to rest under the very same tree where his grandfather once had napped. Like his grandfather, the young man fell asleep and woke to find that all the laboriously woven hats had vanished. He looked here and there without any idea what could have become of them. Suddenly he remembered a story that his grandfather had often told him when he was just a boy. So he looked up into the tree, and sure enough, there sat a band of monkeys with broad grins on their faces and straw hats on their heads.

The young man took off his hat, examined it briefly, and put it back on.

The monkeys did the same.

The young hat maker then fanned himself theatrically with his hat. Again the monkeys screeched, swung about in the branches, and imitated the man.

The grandson confidently took his hat in hand a third time. He held it high for all to see. The monkeys watched with bated breath. The young man exaggerated a look of disgust and called loudly: "I do not like this hat at all anymore." With that he flung the hat energetically into the grass.

High above him the monkeys burst into laughter. They shrieked and bared their teeth, they thrashed around in the treetop, they threw their hats into the air, and they caught them again. Not a single monkey threw his hat to the ground.

The young man stood helpless at the foot of the tree. Then he saw one of the monkeys climbing down to him. With one final leap the animal landed right in front of him. "You have a grandfather who told you tales and taught you a trick or two," he said with a broad grin, "but we monkeys have grandfathers, too!"

Three Women and One Man

There once lived a handsome young man who was known about town for his intelligence, affability, and wit. He came from a well-to-do family and would have enjoyed a carefree childhood but for his fear of snakes. Any time he happened upon a snake, be it ever so small and harmless, he would run home screaming, and there was little anyone could do to console him. At night he would dream that cobras and vipers were chasing him. No matter how fast he ran, they always caught him and bit him.

Nor did marriage do anything to temper his fear. Time and again he swore to his wife that he would one day die of a snake bite. But she must not have him cremated, as was the custom. She must instead tie him to a raft and allow him to drift downriver to the sea.

One day his wife heard a terrible cry from the garden. She rushed out only to find her husband lying motionless on the path while a venomous snake slithered away through the grass. The woman broke into a loud lamentation and sent for a carpenter so that at least she might honor her husband's dying wish. The craftsman built the raft, and amid many tears the young man was sent on his final journey.

Downstream there lived a snake charmer with his three daughters, who happened to be swimming and playing in the water just as the body floated past. "Look, a raft with a corpse," cried the eldest. Her sister swam out and pulled with all her might to bring the raft ashore. The youngest of the three ran home to fetch their father. Upon examining the lifeless body, the snake charmer noticed the bite and declared to his daughters that the young man was not dead and that he could save him. They dragged him to their nearby hut, where the father drew the poison from the wound and rubbed the young man's chest with his ointments. Soon enough the seemingly dead man came back to his senses. The three sisters fell in love with him at first sight, and there followed an energetic argument about who should be allowed to marry him.

"He belongs to me," insisted the first. "I am the one who spotted him floating in the river."

"Nonsense," spat the second. "If it hadn't been for me pulling him to shore, he would not be with us at all. I have the right to be his wife."

"Ridiculous," objected the third. "If I hadn't fetched our father he would have died before our eyes. I should be the one to marry him."

The sisters' quarrel got nastier and nastier until the eldest finally called an end to it. "There are many young men. Let's be done fighting. If we can't agree, then let him go his own way."

The middle sister agreed, but the youngest did not. "If none of us can have him, then no one at all shall marry him," she cried, and in the blink of an eye she slipped a magical ribbon over the ankle of the startled young man. All at once he transformed into a beautiful parrot and flew away.

In his search for food, the parrot chanced to land in the king's garden. It was a sprawling park with numerous magnificent flowers that the bird plucked one after the other. The furious gardener tried to drive him off with a few stones, but he was a poor shot and every one of them went wide of its mark. Eventually he managed to lure the bird into a trap. He brought him to the king and reported in a fluster what this good-for-nothing parrot had done. Then he asked for permission to kill him.

The king, however, took a shine to the handsome animal with his brilliant plumage. He commanded that a golden cage be prepared for the bird, and he presented it to his daughter. The young princess was immediately smitten with the parrot. She was bored to death of her lavishly appointed tower chamber, and she passed many hours of the day engaged with her new companion. She taught him a few words and tamed him so that he would sit on her shoulder and eat from her hand.

One day she noticed a small yellow ribbon on his foot. Curious, she untied it, and before her eyes the bird transformed into the handsome young man he had previously been. The two fell in love at once, and so began a months-long affair that was as passionate as it was secret. As soon as anyone approached the princess's chamber she would tie the magic ribbon around his foot and he would turn again into the parrot.

Eventually the chambermaids grew suspicious of the loud and joyful sounds that would emanate at times from the princess's room. They crept to the door and spied through the keyhole. A young man! In the princess's bedroom! The gentlewomen's cries of dismay resounded through the palace. Prepared to kill an intruder, the palace guard hurried to the scene and thoroughly searched the princess's chamber, but they found only the king's daughter and her parrot. The bird was so agitated that the commandant decided to take a closer look. Before he could seize it, however, the parrot flew into the air and darted about the room. Alarmed by the soldiers' sharp lances, it screeched loudly and disappeared out the window.

Everything might have turned out all right, had not the parrot's ribbon caught on a hook in the window frame. The ribbon came loose and the parrot transformed before their eyes into a young man. He fell into a bush at the base of the tower, where he lay stunned but mercifully uninjured. Hearing the cries of the fast-approaching soldiers, he sprang to his feet and dashed off.

He was fleet of foot, but his pursuers were unrelenting. Gradually his strength began to wane, and he looked desperately for someplace to hide. He spotted a villa in the distance and made for it as fast as his feet would carry him. He burst through the door, disrupting a wealthy merchant at lunch with his wife and daughter.

"You must save me," the young man pleaded. "The king's soldiers are after me, but I've done nothing wrong."

The host knew from his own experience that the king was not always just. "Sit down at the table, and act as if you are one of us," he said, setting an extra place for the stranger.

Not long after, the palace guard burst through the door. "We are looking for an intruder," they shouted, "and we saw him run into this house."

"We didn't notice anything, but feel free to look around," replied the merchant. "In the meantime, please allow my wife, my daughter, my son-in-law, and me to finish our meal in peace."

The soldiers turned the whole house upside down, but because they had not seen their quarry's face, they never suspected a thing. Eventually they apologized for the disturbance and continued their search elsewhere.

The daughter, on the other hand, had fallen head-over-heels in love with the visitor, and she asked her parents for permission to marry him. They were inclined to honor their only child's every wish, and since the young man did not object, they were married a few days later.

As for the princess, her heart was broken. She ceased to speak, eat, or drink, and she fell quite ill. Her father summoned the most renowned healers in the entire realm, but no one knew what was wrong with her or how to ease her suffering. The king came to his daughter and ordered the others to leave the room. "Dearest," he began, "you are the most important thing in the world to me. Tell me, is there truly nothing I can do for you?"

At that the princess broke down and told him all that had happened and how her heart would fall to pieces if she could never see her beloved again.

The king knew just what to do. He commanded that the royal theater stage a performance, to which he invited all the leading families and nobles in his realm. Anyone who refused the invitation would face a severe punishment.

During the performance the princess went through the aisles closely examining each guest. It was not long before she found her lover and his new bride. "You have stolen my man," shrieked the furious princess.

"It would seem that he left you," the young bride replied coolly. "He's with me now."

Just then another woman leapt up and declared that this man was her dead husband, and that he belonged to her.

The quarrel gathered energy until the king called upon the highest judge in the land for help.

The judge listened to each woman's story, and after careful consideration, issued this decision: "The first woman thought her husband was dead, and she gave him up to the river. At that moment their marriage was over.

The princess then lived with him in a marriage-like relationship. She freed him from his curse and cared for him. But she did not protect him when her father's soldiers hunted and tried to kill him. For that reason she, too, has no legitimate claim. The rich merchant's daughter and her family, on the other hand, provided him sanctuary. Without her help he would have been captured and executed by the soldiers. She is, therefore, his only rightful wife."

The Story of the Father and His Son,
Or Where the Wind and Water Got Their Power

There was once a couple who lived in a village and wished more than anything for a child. They practiced patience, as the neighbors suggested. They drank the teas the herbalist brewed for them. They tried on the days the astrologer recommended.

All for naught.

They had nearly abandoned hope when the woman became pregnant after all and gave birth to a son. It was the most beautiful day in her husband's life. He could not take his eyes off the miracle in his arms. The baby was very big, much bigger and stronger than other infants. The man did not mind. "Every child is different," he informed the astonished neighbors.

Nor was he surprised when the child uttered his first words after only a few hours. "I am hungry," the lad cried loudly and clearly.

"He has a healthy appetite," the father said as he started to feed his son. And the boy never stopped eating. At one month old he would eat more for breakfast than three other children would eat in a day. By one year old he was insatiable, eating enough rice and vegetables at a single meal to satisfy an entire family.

"There's something wrong with that kid," the neighbors whispered, eyeing him with suspicion. But the parents loved their son above all else and would not hear any of it. Even when the young boy started to grow beyond all proportion, they did not mind in the least. "Every child is different," the father repeated again and again.

When the five-year-old boy towered head and shoulders over his parents, his own mother began to find him unsettling.

"He frightens me," she told her husband one evening while the boy was asleep.

"Don't you get started with that nonsense," the father replied, incensed. "He is our beloved son; let him eat and grow as much as he likes."

To keep the child from starving, the father got up before the sun each day to work his fields, and he was happy to do it. But even as the boy matured there was no indication that his growth or appetite was slowing down, and the father was starting to worry. He had to admit that he and his wife were no longer the youngest and that their energy was gradually flagging. How much longer could they hope to keep their child's hunger at bay, especially when he seemed disinclined to lend a hand in the fields?

So the father and son had a serious talk: "My dear boy, you are so big and strong, and your parents are getting weary from all the work. It's time for you to help us out."

"Of course!" the boy replied: "I would be delighted. Just tell me what I can do, and I'll take care of it."

The father, much relieved, explained to him that in the coming weeks a section of the forest would have to be cleared to make room for new fields. The next day he went to the village smith and bought a new ax. He gave it to his son, who smiled at him indulgently. "My honored father, what should I do with such a small tool? Get me a respectable ax so that I can help you properly."

The man went back to the smith and purchased the largest ax. Yet this tool, too, looked like a toy in his son's mighty hands. In the end the smith forged an ax so big and heavy that he could move it only with the help of two journeymen.

"This one is just right," the son cried, elated. "Now, dear father, show me the trees you want me to cut down."

The two set out in good spirits. The farmer was hoping to clear a sizable area, and he expected it would take weeks. The son, on the other hand, seemed unimpressed by the amount of work before them. "Father, you have worked so much for my sake. Go home and rest. I'll get started, and you can check on my progress this evening."

The father was not entirely comfortable with the prospect of leaving his child alone, be he ever so big and strong. But his joints ached, and he was exhausted and grateful for the offer.

When he returned in the afternoon, not one tree was down, and his son was nowhere in sight. Filled with dread, he ran through the wood in search of him and found him asleep in a clearing, his head nestled on a boulder. The father gazed tenderly at his sleeping son. True, he was a giant, but he was also still a child, and a sweet one at that. Even with all the work that lay before them, he could not bring himself to wake the lad. Soon enough the boy woke on his own and flinched at the sight of his father. "I am so sorry. I was a little sleepy, and I thought I would rest a bit. Now I've slept the whole day away. Forgive me."

"Don't worry," the father answered lovingly. "We'll just start tomorrow. It's too late for today. Let's go home. I'm sure you're hungry."

"No, no. You go ahead. I'll get started on the work and join you later."

"But it'll be dark soon."

"No matter. Don't worry about a thing."

"Parents always worry," the farmer remarked with a smile, then headed home to his wife.

His son, meanwhile, set to work. He was felling trees at lightning speed. A few powerful strokes sufficed to topple the largest of them as if it were a stalk of straw. In no time at all every tree or bush in the vicinity was down. Feeling satisfied, the boy set off for home.

The next morning, when the father saw what his son had accomplished, he nearly burst with pride. He must tell everyone in the village how diligent and helpful his child was. The other farmers were rightly flabbergasted when they saw the trees all chopped down and neatly stacked. But their amazement soon turned to envy and resentment. This giant could knock out in a few easy hours what for them represented weeks of drudgery. Imagine what he could do when it came to planting and harvesting! The old farmer and his wife needed hardly lift a finger, and still they would soon be among the wealthiest in the village.

And so they began to sow the seeds of doubt and fear. They took every opportunity to warn the old farmer about his child. He was a giant with superhuman strength, and still he was growing and getting stronger. For now he was gentle and good-natured, but what if he became aggressive or ill-tempered as a young man or even turned against his mother and father? No one would be able to stop him. He was a threat to the entire village, not least of all his parents. It was high time to be rid of him.

The father refused to listen to such prattle. It was nothing but chatty nonsense. He loved his son far too much to think even for a second of sending him away.

When the villagers saw how the old man ignored them, they decided to ambush the father and son and kill them. They invited them both to join them on a hunt. The father hoped it might be the end of their animosity, and the son was always willing to help, so they both accepted without a second thought.

A couple of the farmers sent the two ahead into a ravine that was known for treacherous rockslides. Meanwhile, the others were doing all they could to trigger an avalanche. They were able to get a few fragments of rock rolling. Those drew others in their wake, and they all bore deafeningly down on the father and son. One swift leap brought the father to safety behind a cliff face, but the son stood there calmly. He caught the largest boulder and lugged it back to the village. It was so heavy that ten men would not have been able to carry it. The lad set it down, but not carefully enough, so that it started to roll. It thundered right through the village, leaving a trail of devastation. Huts, houses, stables—nothing that stood in its path was left unscathed. By some miracle no one was killed, but several pigs, cows, and calves were dead.

The villagers were outraged. Had they not warned the old man? Had they not pointed out the danger the boy giant posed? It was only by chance that no lives were lost. Next time they would not be so lucky. And now it really was time to be rid of that child once and for all.

The old man had no idea what to do. He loved his son, but maybe the villagers were right: It was only a matter of time before the boy would cause some dreadful calamity with his unbelievable strength. Full of despair, he tried for days to come up with some solution, but nothing came to mind.

"What's troubling you?" the son asked. "Can I do anything to help?"

"No," replied the father, and his heart clenched into a knot.

In the end he bade his child follow him into the woods to help him fell a tree. When they had found one with a massive trunk, he suggested that they first take a little rest. Within minutes the son had fallen asleep, and the father set to work on the tree so that it would crush the child when it fell. At the last stroke, as the tree began to fall, the child woke and just managed to dodge the falling monstrosity.

"Why didn't you wake me?" he asked innocently. "I would have been happy to do that for you." He shouldered the massive trunk and dragged it to the village, where he dropped it so clumsily in the family's yard that the massive boughs and crown utterly destroyed the house and stable.

By this time the father, too, recognized that his son posed a danger to others. But he would never be able to kill him himself.

At the urging of the other villagers he resorted to a trick. He claimed to be suffering severe stomach pains, which, according to the healer, could be alleviated only by a serving of tiger meat. The son set out at once to hunt the predator and returned a few hours later with his kill.

Now the father claimed also to need the blood of at least half a dozen cobras. Once again the son set out, and within a short time he stood in the door, six dead snakes in hand. "I hope you get well soon. Is there anything else I can do for you?"

The father asked for a *khonran*, a bird as rare as it was dangerous, and his loyal and credulous son set out at once. He strayed for days through the forests without finding a single trace of the bird. He wandered farther, climbed trees and hills; for his father he would leave no stone unturned. On the fifth day, high atop a towering tree, he finally discovered a *khonran* nest. He scrambled up, but it was empty. Patiently he awaited the bird's return.

In the meantime the father was suffering from a guilty conscience. How could he have listened to the other villagers? How could he have dreamed up such a wicked trick? Risking the life of a good-natured son to cure a father's imaginary illness? And so he set out to look for his child. After a long search he found him in the crown of a tree. Just as he was about to call his name, two *khonrans* flew into view. With a mighty blow the boy killed one of them, but the other flew high into the sky, then dove straight down at the intruder and drove its long hard beak into the boy's heart.

With a great clatter the son fell from the tree and landed at his father's feet. "Oh, Father, I'm about to die. Tell me, where should I put my strength?"

The old man's heart was breaking. "My son, forgive me. Give your strength to the water and your breath to the wind."

The Long Path to Wisdom

Long ago there lived a mother and father who had only one child, whom they loved above all else. The well-to-do family lived in a lavish villa, and wanted for nothing. Even so, they worried constantly about their son, and were very protective of him. For fear of sickness and bad influences they forbade all contact with other children. The boy's teachers came to the house, and otherwise the parents and the servants tended to his every need. The parents believed their child was leading a life free of care, but they failed to notice how lonely he was. When he got bored, which happened often, he would run through the garden startling birds or hunting insects and geckos, until that, too, grew wearisome.

One day he could stand it no longer; he slipped unseen out of the gate and into the street in search of diversion. He discovered many things that were strange to him, and he marveled at them. Three evenings in a row he watched the comings and goings, and he noticed that each night many of the people were walking in the same direction. His curiosity eventually got the better of his trepidation, and he asked a passerby what all the fuss was about. The stranger told him that the people were going to listen to the sermons of a famous monk who had many things to say about the teachings of the Buddha and about how to lead a moral life. This was exciting news for a boy who until then had known only his parents' house!

The very next evening he went to the monastery and hung on the monk's every word. He was immediately swept away! That benevolent voice spoke with such wisdom and serenity. He knew at once that his only purpose from then on was to become a novice, to follow the path of the Buddha and to seek enlightenment. Anxiously he ran home to beg his parents to send him to the monastery. Any feelings of shame he might have had about his unsanctioned forays into the world were quickly forgotten.

His mother and father listened to him sadly and shook their heads. The request seemed to them the mere folly of a child who had ventured for the first time into the dangerous, filthy, seductive world. What's more, he was their only son, and they had no desire to let him go. They needed him so that he could marry and carry on the family, and so that he could care for them when they grew old. The boy was crestfallen. The monastery would not accept him without his parents' permission. He begged and pleaded, but all in vain. His parents stood their ground.

Full of disappointment, the boy withdrew. He stopped talking to his parents. He would neither eat nor drink. He lay in bed sad and angry, and he refused to get up. Over the course of six days the already lean child grew thinner and thinner despite his parents' perpetual pleas.

On the seventh day, the father said to his wife: "We are afraid of losing our child to the monastery, but the way things are going we'll lose him a different way. We can't let our son starve!" The mother agreed that they could not go on like that. Quietly they walked into their son's darkened room and told him the news. Forgetting all his weariness and exhaustion, the boy leapt from his bed and ran to the monastery, where they shaved his head, and he donned the robes of a novice.

He stayed with the monks for several years, and everyone praised the devoted, perceptive, and studious young man he became. He was the most disciplined at meditation, the most diligent at the daily chores, and the most knowledgeable in the discussions of the Eightfold Path, the Five Moral Precepts, and the Four Noble Truths. As time went by, however, he noticed that in the hustle and bustle of the monastery he was not coming any closer to his higher goals of wisdom, inner peace, and absolute clarity of mind in meditation. He discussed this with his master, an older monk, who sent him into the forest, where he could train his spirit and continue his studies far removed from all distractions.

The young monk lived a long time in the woods devoting himself fervently to his goals, yet even after twelve years in the solitude of nature, his desire for enlightenment was still unfulfilled. To be sure, he knew a great deal about the Buddha's teachings, but his thoughts were too scattered, fragmented, unfocused. He was too restless.

The dejected monk gave up his search and took the road back to the monastery. He had no idea what he would do next. Along the way he met his former master, the old monk, who told him a story of a previously wealthy but now impoverished couple whose son had left them many years ago to enter a monastery. The two must have bad karma, the old man sighed. After the son left, the servants had taken to stealing valuables from the house, and then the family had lent money to various parties who subsequently disappeared without a trace. Victims of lamentable circumstances, the couple were now advanced in age and could no longer work. To make matters worse, the son who might have cared for them was gone.

Full of foreboding, the young monk set out to find the elderly couple. Could it be his own parents? Along the way he passed by a familiar monastery. The words of a sermon drifted into the street from somewhere inside. He hesitated. Monks were not allowed to have close contact with their families, much less to care for them. The young man found himself confronted with a difficult choice: Should he lay aside his robe and search for his parents or should he abandon his parents and remain in the monastery?

The young man put this question to the Buddha in prayer, and to his surprise it seemed to him that the Buddha answered. He advised him to remain a monk, but to seek his parents and to find a way to integrate these two aspects of his life. Relieved, he contemplated this as he continued on his way.

When he came to the place where his childhood home had stood, he saw nothing but a field of refuse where a few cows grazed. Even at a distance he could make out two elderly individuals sitting by the side of the road. They crouched down in the customary posture of deference as the unknown monk approached them. Touched and ashamed, he recognized his mother and father at once. They had grown old and looked wretched.

Overwhelmed by emotion, the son stood before his kneeling parents. He wept bitterly and could not bring himself to speak. But a few of the tears dripped from his cheek and fell on his mother's exposed neck. Puzzled, she looked up and recognized the son she thought she had lost.

All three now wept tears of joy and embraced warmly. The son made countless apologies for having left his parents, but they would not hear it. All was forgiven and forgotten. Together they discussed what was to be done, and in the end the monk found a place in the vicinity of the monastery for his parents to live. In the days that followed he shared with them the food he collected as part of his daily alms. Again he conversed with the Buddha. Was this infraction of the rules and norms allowed? The Buddha reassured him and even permitted him to divert donations of clothing intended for the monks to his needy parents.

The other monks eyed the young man suspiciously. He would often disappear with alms and offerings only to return later without them. Finally, the incensed monks demanded he explain himself. At that moment the Buddha intervened and spoke to them: Respect for one's parents and a readiness to help the needy are the supreme virtues, he declared. It is not enough to lead a contemplative Buddhist life; one must also put teachings into practice. As in the pagoda, so in the home.

And so it happened that the son cared for his parents till the end of their days and then eventually returned with a pure heart to the forest, where his childhood dream came true and he finally attained enlightenment.

Epilogue

∙∙∙∙∙∙∙∙∙∙∙∙∙∙∙

JAN-PHILIPP SENDKER

Since my first trip to Burma in May 1995, I have traveled to the country about two dozen times—first as a journalist and later in order to research my novels and to see friends. Over the first few years little changed from one visit to the next. The short flight from Bangkok always felt like a journey back in time. At the airport there was the same little terminal. The streets of Yangon were pitted with potholes. The familiar rusty, dented cars shared the lanes with children playing soccer. Old buildings crumbled; construction sites were as rare as new businesses; the power went out several times a day.

A military junta continued to rule the country, which remained an economic and political pariah. The Western sanctions were still in place, and even tourists gave the former British colony a wide berth. The violently suppressed uprising by the monks in the fall of 2007, the destructive cyclone Nargis one year later, and the military's refusal to accept foreign help finished the job of isolating Burma. Years passed. A crippling standstill prevailed across a country that seemed frozen in time. While in other parts of the world the Internet was accelerating the pace of change, here there were few computers and even fewer mobile phones.

In the fall of 2011, for the first time in decades, parliamentary elections were held. They were, however, neither fair nor free, and were consequently boycotted by the opposition. To no one's surprise, the military party won and the former general Thein Sein was elected president. Just when it seemed as if Burma's future would be no different from its past, something suddenly happened that no one had anticipated. Thein Sein cautiously opened a dialogue with Aung San Suu Kyi, the opposition leader under house arrest. An economic and political reform process was set in motion, at first slowly, but then gaining in momentum. Political prisoners were released, censorship was eased, and opposition parties were permitted. In response the West gradually reversed its sanctions until they were all but completely lifted.

During those years I could see subtle changes on every visit. Traffic picked up slightly; new private airlines sprang up; the first large supermarkets opened their doors. I noticed an increasing number of mobile phone users. The price of a SIM card dropped from several thousand U.S. dollars to just a few hundred. Tea shops were decorated with flags of the NLD opposition party, waitresses wore T-shirts bearing the likeness of Aung San Suu Kyi. The joy and pride in their faces were harbingers of the even more radical political and social changes to come.

In the fall of 2015 the political spring led to the first free elections in almost thirty years. The opposition won in a landslide, but still had limited powers. The constitution guarantees the military 25 percent of parliamentary seats and three of the most important ministries.

Even so, the country was changing from visit to visit at a pace I had only ever witnessed in China.

Burma, early 2017: Even as I land in Yangon the differences are striking. In the outlying districts of the city, one finds the first heralds of globalization: factories emerging out of thin air with their red, blue, or green metallic roofs, beside them long rows of apartment blocks for the workers. Not far off are the rich relatives of the factories: designer neighborhoods of cookie-cutter, single-family homes for the well-to-do. In the distance one can make out the first hints of something like a Yangon skyline:

isolated skyscrapers towering up into the air. On the tarmac stand planes from Singapore and Dubai. There is a multistory terminal with arrival and departure gates. As I go through customs I present the electronic visa that I applied for online.

The city center is no longer just twenty minutes away; now it takes over an hour and a half. Traffic. The air quality is poor; the city is draped in smog. There is a construction site on every corner. There are new hotels, shopping centers, and car dealers. Yangon's answer to Rodeo Drive is soon to open, and the billboards promise an excess of "luxury and elegance." Close at hand is a large Mercedes dealership.

I think with longing of the time years ago when my driver thought "McDonald's" might be a Scottish gentleman, when a mere handful of cars used the streets, and when it took only twenty minutes to get to my downtown hotel. Of course I recognize that it was pleasant for me back then because I happened to be sitting in one of the few cars on the road. I would probably have found the situation much less romantic if I had needed to carry my luggage from the airport to town in the hundred-degree heat, or if I had been riding on one of the few and crowded buses.

Little has changed at the hotel in the past few years, aside from the price. Sometimes it skyrockets exorbitantly;

other times it crashes suddenly. It is not always easy to discern the patterns in the Burmese markets.

I take a walk through Yangon's old center. It is at once familiar and strange. The streets are full of people, chaotic and loud. It is hot, as always in the spring. Vendors have spread their vegetables or books out on the sidewalks. People sit chatting on the stoops; the side streets are full of little restaurants, food stalls, and tea shops. The guests squat on the streets as they have always done, drinking coffee or tea, conversing, watching the hubbub around them or checking their mobile phones. Of the country's fifty-three million inhabitants, thirty-five million reportedly own a cell phone. Ten million Burmese are on Facebook. Every third shop, it seems, is selling phones. I buy a SIM card for the equivalent of five dollars and next thing I know I am sitting in a vaulted arcade sipping Burmese tea and checking my emails from Germany.

I find myself wondering if a country so long isolated, a society so shaped by tradition, can cope with the sudden and unmitigated onslaught of capitalism, the enticing promises of materialism, without being fundamentally altered.

The next day, as on every trip, I pay a visit to the Bagan Book Shop on Thirty-Seventh Street. Sadly, the owner, my friend, died a few years ago. Since then his son has been running the business. He is sitting in the shop with two friends. One is playing guitar. In the middle of it all is a television playing a South Korean soap opera.

Books are no longer restored here.

He greets me warmly and we are chatting about an old Rangoon guidebook when his daughter suddenly comes into the shop. She is twenty-four years old and I ask whether she ever read any of the books that her grandfather so painstakingly restored. "Only a couple," she confesses, and tells me that next week she will be leaving to spend three years in Papua New Guinea because she has found work there in a supermarket.

I am flabbergasted. To me it seems that Yangon is in the midst of an economic boom; surely there must be plenty of work here for young people. She sighs. It's true, but the jobs here pay so poorly that she would rather work abroad. Besides, her grandfather always wanted her to be able to get out and discover the world for herself. Now it's finally possible.

Suddenly the ceiling lights flicker a few times, then go out. The television is silent. A blackout. Even now, a daily irritation. But no one lights any candles. In just a moment, the power is back on. Outside the shop you can hear the dull droning of a motor. It comes from one of the emergency generators you can now see everywhere on the streets.

That evening I am sitting somewhere on Nineteenth Street eating grilled vegetables and watching the Burmese diners around me playing on their phones or avidly following the English Premier League's game of the season on a large flat-screen on the wall.

A land in transition. And yet there are facets that remain completely untouched. The national railroad, for instance. At the main station in Yangon, a man still writes the schedule by hand on a large board with a black felt-tip pen. There are no computers for tickets; they, too, are still handwritten. The journey from Yangon to Kalaw is less than four hundred miles, but it takes twenty-two hours and costs about twelve dollars. The travel time is longer than it was eighty years ago. It seems unlikely that there are many other train lines in the world that have actually gotten slower over the last several decades.

The "night train to Mandalay" leaves the station at 5:00 p.m. sharp. As on my first journey twenty-two years ago we lumber along at ten, sometimes twenty miles per hour. Sometimes we go no faster than a walk. Warm air wafts in through the open windows. Street vendors scurry up to the train and hop on. They pass through the cars hawking curries, tea, or soup in plastic bags, fruit, crackers, water. At some point they just jump off again.

Rice paddies, narrow rivers, and children riding water buffalo roll past my window. The sun sets behind palm trees.

It is the ideal speed for the human senses. I hear the voices of children playing, but the scent of open cooking fires is less prominent. There are more streetlights now, and in the darkness lamplight shines from most of the huts. The economic development of recent years has brought electricity to many villages—electricity and trash. The country is fast on its way to becoming a dump. Everything that was previously wrapped in leaves or cloth is now packaged in plastic, the more the better, which is then carelessly thrown away. Considering that trash removal is available in very few cities, the people simply do not know what to do with all the plastic. They toss it into ponds and rivers, along streets and paths, or into their backyards. The sight of the landscape teeming with blue, green, or white plastic bags is sometimes hard to bear.

When I get to Kalaw, a friend asks me amazed why I subjected myself to the uncomfortable and tedious train ride. The flight would have taken only an hour. Or I could have taken one of the modern air-conditioned buses that now connect the country's cities. In his eyes, I am an incurable romantic wallowing in nostalgia. I object. The train is neither comfortable nor efficient, but it offers the best opportunity to glimpse a different, more intimate side of the country.

Kalaw is changing, too. Tourists have discovered it. Instead of four hotels there are now about forty establishments ready to welcome guests, and more are under construction. There is a Mexican restaurant called Picasso and an Italian restaurant with a pizza oven and mozzarella on the menu. Many of the streets are freshly paved; there is a brand-new municipal trash collection service; traffic is picking up; mopeds have replaced the last horse-drawn carriages. And the property values have gone through the roof. Given its pleasant climate at an altitude of about forty-five hundred feet, the little city is a popular destination for the Burmese themselves. A friend tells me that a piece of land ten thousand square feet can cost half a million U.S. dollars. Come again? Half a million dollars? In Kalaw? He nods. Black-market cash. The military leaders have to sink their ill-gotten fortunes into something, after all.

That afternoon I stroll through a little park downtown, and just as before some young people are sitting under the pines, playing guitar and singing. They laugh and wave to me and invite me to sing along.

A few days later we visit a monastery in the vicinity of Taunggyi. An abbot founded it more than ten years ago and it has since grown to be one of the largest in Burma, financed entirely by private donations. It houses 650 novices, the youngest of them under age ten. On a separate campus there are about a thousand girls who are also able to attend the monastery school. Most of the young people and children come from the nearby Pa-O villages. On the walls of the abbot's office hang class schedules and excerpts of lesson plans. They reveal an ambitious curriculum. Above all he wants to teach the children to think and act critically and independently. Psychology is one of the subjects, alongside Environmental Protection and History and Culture of the Pa-O.

"Do the folk tales of the Pa-O play any kind of role?" I ask, hoping to collect a new story or two.

"Folk tales?" The abbot wrinkles his brow, then smiles. "Hardly. We have trouble enough getting the kids to put their smartphones down. They're forbidden in the monastery, but we see their influence. The students today lack concentration and are more easily

distracted than ten years ago. Folk tales hold little interest for them, I fear."

At the end of my journey I have a kind of reading in
Yangon. My two Burma novels, having recently been
released in Burmese, have found a wide readership. The
publisher has organized an event with the press and a
public audience. We are sitting in a café with a gallery in
the city center. About forty people have turned up; aside
from me hardly anyone is over thirty. I feel uncertain. I
have no sense of how long I should speak, because I have
no idea whether anyone will be willing to ask questions
at the end. My publisher says to keep it short and not
to worry.

I talk a little bit about how the novels came to be
and then ask if anyone has any questions. Several hands
shoot immediately into the air. And that is just the beginning. For two hours we discuss the books, Burma, and the
process of writing novels. Their curiosity and thirst for
knowledge know no bounds.

We even discuss the crimes of the military and the
deployment of young men to clear land mines, a circumstance that plays a prominent role in the novel *A Well-
Tempered Heart*. A woman stands up and asks me whether

this is something I invented or whether it is based on fact. For a moment I am unsure what to say. It is not so long ago that the novel would never have been allowed in Burma and the young woman would have spent years in prison merely for asking such a question.

She is waiting for my answer.

I take a deep breath and tell her about the interviews I conducted years ago with men who had suffered these tortures. These stories were true, and the atrocities committed by the soldiers were probably much worse than I portrayed them. And while I am saying this and looking into the open, inquisitive faces before me, I decide that problems such as traffic jams and rubbish heaps are much less dire in the context of the triumph represented by the people's release from fear.

Back in Yangon, shortly before my departure, I visit Than Htlun, a dealer in books and antiques who has been running a little shop in Scott Market for decades. Business has not been bad, he says. Thanks to the influx of tourists the demand for old Burmese handcrafts has grown, though good pieces are hard to come by. These days you have to travel to the remotest villages, and the prices get higher from week to week.

He invites me to dinner at his home that evening. His wife, Mimi, makes some delicious Burmese dishes. There are curries and Burmese wine.

I tell him about my journey and my observations and I ask him to recommend books about Burma and its culture in light of the changes in recent years. With the slightest hesitation he pulls three dusty old volumes of Burmese folk tales off the shelf.

"But these are all folk tales," I object, surprised.

"I know," he replies with a laugh. "It doesn't matter. Folk tales reveal a lot about a country and its people, its culture, its values."

"And what about all the changes I've encountered during my visit?"

There are no books about that yet, he tells me, and say what you like about Facebook, the change has not begun to affect the old roots of the culture. "Every country changes, Burma included. It was changing before, too, though more slowly. There was a time when the men covered their bodies with tattoos and wore their hair in long braids. Neither is the practice now. What matters is deeper than that. And the soul of a people, as it is described in folk tales, does not change so quickly."

Yangon, spring of 2017

Acknowledgments

································

Numerous people have helped us with our research in Burma in various ways over the years. We are deeply indebted to all of them. Without them this book would not exist.

Particular thanks go to Winston and Tommy in Kalaw.

Ma Ei, Hans Leiendecker, and Bert Morsbach at the Aythaya Winery have generously and repeatedly supported Jonathan and Janek for months at a time.

Yeyint Kyaw, Tin Htun Aung, and Nee Nee Myint provided Lorie Karnath invaluable service as translators.

Ursula Bischoff translated Lorie's texts into German.

Maung Htin Aung, the former rector of the University of Yangon, engaged deeply with the folklore of his country and published collections of Burmese tales in the forties and fifties of the previous century. These, too, were a source and inspiration for us.

Authors

JAN-PHILIPP SENDKER is an internationally bestselling author born in Hamburg in 1960. He was the American correspondent for *Stern* from 1990 to 1995, and its Asian correspondent from 1995 to 1999. In 2000 he published *Cracks in the Wall*, a nonfiction book about China. His first novel, *The Art of Hearing Heartbeats* (Other Press), is an international bestseller, and the sequel, *A Well-Tempered Heart* (Other Press), appeared in 2014. His third novel in the Heartbeats trilogy is set to be published in 2019. He lives in Berlin with his family.

LORIE KARNATH is an author, explorer, and lecturer. She was the thirty-seventh president of The Explorers Club, and founded The Explorers Museum, a not-for-profit entity dedicated to preserving and fostering scientific exploration and discovery. She has written numerous books and articles on the sciences, exploration, and the arts.

JONATHAN SENDKER spent a gap year in Myanmar, traveling, doing volunteer work, and collecting stories for this book. He now studies Liberal Arts & Sciences in Utrecht, the Netherlands.

Translators

LISA LIESENER has been translating for almost twenty years and took special pleasure in embarking on a journey filled with spirits, dragons, and talking animals. She holds an engineering degree from the University of Applied Sciences in Stuttgart, Germany, and currently directs children's programs for a nonprofit organization she cofounded to promote education and connection with the natural world. She lives in Connecticut with her family.

KEVIN WILIARTY has a BA in German from Harvard and a PhD from the University of California, Berkeley. A native of the United States, he has also lived in Germany and Japan. He is currently a Web developer at Hampshire College in Amherst, Massachusetts. He lives in Connecticut with his wife and two children, and also plays bass in a string band.

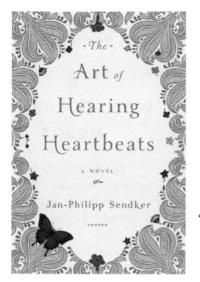

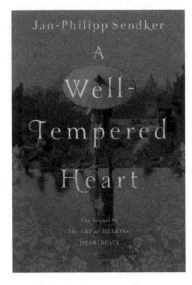